INVADING
TIBET

INVADING TIBET

TIBET

———◆———

MARK FRUTKIN

SOHO

I would like to thank the Ontario Arts Council for a
Works-in-progress grant during the writing of this book
and the Canada Council for their support.

Published in the United States of America by
Soho Press Inc.
853 Broadway
New York, NY 10003

Published in Canada by Random House of Canada, Ltd.

Library of Congress Cataloging-in-Publication Data

Frutkin, Mark, 1948–
Invading Tibet/Mark Frutkin.
p.   cm.
ISBN 0-939149-74-5
1. British—China—Tibet—History—20th century—Fiction.
I. Title.
PR9199.3.F776I58   1993   92-31225
813'.54—dc20   CIP

Manufactured in the United States
10 9 8 7 6 5 4 3 2 1

Already a fictitious past occupies in our memories the place of another, a past of which we know nothing with certainty — not even that it is false.

Jorge Luis Borges, *Tlon, Ugbar, Orbis Tertius*

To the People of Tibet

CHAPTER I

1.

Montreal, 1985

"Time, gentlemen..." Milton and I had finished our drinks and were on our way out of the half-empty bar, a small English-style pub favoured by journalists and media people who worked in the area at the foot of the mountain. We paid our bill and walked into the night.

Rags of fog, ash-coloured, drifted under streetlights. Few cars passed to disturb the dripping silence. Moisture gathered on our faces as we walked the dozen blocks to our respective apartments, first along the base of Mont Royal, then climbing.

We stood outside the door to his place, a basement apartment in a grand old house. The fog softened nearby lights, giving them hazy yellow aureoles.

"I can't believe you're really doing it," said Milton. "I never thought you'd give up that plum job at the university."

"You know you spend years trying to reach some goal, and when you finally reach it you wonder if it was all worthwhile. Time to move on," I shrugged. "What else can you do when you've come to a dead end?"

"But why do you want to write a book about Tibet? What's the guy's name — Chandler?"

"Not Chandler, Candler," I enunciated. I had told Milton earlier about my great-great-uncle, a correspondent who went into Tibet when British and Indian troops invaded in 1904. A mysterious man, part of the familial folklore which is always more myth than fact. I explained that I wanted to find out how much his story was embellished and how much was real, if, in fact, I could even distinguish those threads.

Removing a flat box of Balkan Sobranie from his pocket, Milton opened it, chose a cigarette and placed it in his mouth. It was the only time I had ever seen him smoke. The box disappeared in his gaping pocket and out he came with a pack of matches. I remember thinking that he seemed to be acting in a play. As sometimes happens, when he lit the match a spark flew out, stinging me on the hand. He gazed at the flame as if he were trying to remember something, lit the cigarette, blew smoke into the fog.

"Anyway," Milton continued, "if you're going to do another biography, why don't you do somebody people have heard of — like Churchill, or better yet, Hitler? He's popular."

I knew Milton was playing devil's advocate. "You know I can't do that." Turning, I looked back the way we had come. I thought I heard footsteps approaching through the fog but there was no one. "I feel a powerful connection to Candler — more than just the fact that he's my great-great-uncle. He's starting to haunt me."

Milton shifted, shoved his long hands into the pockets of his raincoat. "What the hell were the Brits doing in Tibet?"

"Because of the Russians," I answered, explaining that the Russians and English were at each other's throats in those days, everyone predicting war. The British thought Tsar Nicholas II was swaying the Dalai Lama to the Russian side, thereby gaining a foothold in Tibet from which they could threaten India. "It was all in their imaginations, of course. Total illusion. Part of the Great Game, as they called international politics in those days."

Milton turned up his collar. "And where did Candler stand in all this?"

"I'm not sure what happened to him there, in the mountains of Tibet, though I remember my grandfather saying that Edmund was a man who had seen too much."

I decided not to tell Milton everything, knowing it would all come out in time, at the right time. But

3

I did mention that Candler, like many of his day, had been fascinated by Tibet, the last of the fabulous lands. Rumours abounded, prompted by the few eccentric travellers who had entered those mountains and returned. Whispers and murmurings in the august halls of the Royal Geographic Society were heard in the furthest reaches of empire. As the British had penetrated the only raw, tangled paradises remaining on the globe — the jungles of Africa and Asia, the Australian outback — so too would they penetrate Tibet. The desire to rend that veil proved irresistible.

"Before Candler even reached Lhasa, the capital," I added, "his adventures were over ... or perhaps they had taken a different direction ..."

"And you think you're going to go back and follow in his footsteps?" Milton asked rhetorically, a mocking severity in his voice.

I stared at him, saying nothing, until he looked at his watch and announced: "Three A.M. I have other fires to tend, Alex. Goodnight."

Walking two blocks through the fog to my own street, I was still bothered by vague questions as I pushed open the door with the diamond-shaped window and climbed the stairs to my cramped attic apartment.

Over the next year, I read everything I could find on Tibet and what was called the Younghusband Expedition, as well as Candler's dispatches, which had been published in the *London Daily Mail*. Eventually, however, I realized I would have to go to London to interview my ancient Aunt Liz, the only remaining member of our family who had actually known Candler. I also wanted to find a private journal of his that I suspected was in the collections of the British Library. When I was ready to leave, a year later, Milton drove me to the airport. "Don't worry," Milton soothed my fears, "I'll get you there on time."

2.

The bartender wiped the counter in wide, easy circles while high above, up against the towering ceiling, stirred giant kites in the shape of monarch butterflies. Migrating passengers hurried through the airport, waited, then hurried again. Milton and I finished our Pernods.

"My best wishes to Candler, when you find him," Milton said, handing me a wrapped gift, badly wrapped in fact, Milton not one to spend precious time on an affair of the hands. Nevertheless, taking it from him, I guessed it was a book. I inspected. Brown paper bag resurrected as wrapping paper. Tape, applied like bandages. White string in crazy orbits.

"I was in a hurry," he answered my questioning look. "Don't open it, Alex, until you are sitting in the reading room of the British Library. All right?"

5

He nodded his long thin head as if asking me to concur and concur I did, nodding back. Stuffing the package into my briefcase of fake black leather, I held out my hand: "Farewell, friend."

Two days later, after having settled into a small hotel in London, I entered the British Museum, the same black bag in my grip. As I climbed the steps, I thought about Edmund Candler and his private journal. Actually, I wasn't sure if there was a journal. I was guessing. But something I had read by Colonel Younghusband mentioned that Candler had written many more dispatches than he sent. I was hoping to find those private dispatches and learn the truth about this strange man, spoken of only in whispers by the elders of the family.

At the top of the steps, I was stopped by a guard standing behind a table. He asked to see my bag. Looking for Irish bombs, I thought, remembering the signs in the tube asking passengers to report any suspicious-looking packages. The kindly, red-faced man rooted about in the bottomless pit of my briefcase. He removed a black Fineliner pen, sniffed it, dropped it back in the bag and moved on to the much more fascinating over-large straw handbag offered by a grey-haired American lady tourist.

Soon I had obtained a three-month pass for research, presented to me by the authorities after I had explained why I wished to enter the inner sanctum. I headed for the reading room itself and was again halted by a guard standing behind a table. This one had a large round head. That was all I noted about him.

As if sticking his hand in a plum pudding, he too searched about in my briefcase and came up with Milton's farewell gift. He stared at it. "What's in this?"

"I believe it's a book. A friend gave it to me as a gift. He asked me not to open it until I was in there." I nodded towards the rotund cavern of the reading room. Its rich, echoey sounds were drifting to me through the double doors. As a worker exited, I glanced in.

"Rather an odd shape for a book," he commented.

"Yes, it is a bit long for a book," I had to admit.

"I will have to have it checked out, sir," said the guard. "Just be a moment, sir." Another of his type took over checking bags as my book disappeared into the bowels of the museum. I sat in a nearby chair, wood polished by many sitters of my sort, and waited patiently.

After about twenty minutes, a third guard, a red-haired woman, replaced the second guard. She saw me waiting. "Can I help you, sir?"

I explained. "He had a large round head," I said to her back as she too vanished into the labyrinth of officialdom. "He's gone to lunch," she said on returning. "I didn't see your package, but why don't you go into the reading room and collect it in an hour or so when he returns?"

I agreed and entered the domed library, anxious to set to work.

Engaging work it was. So engaging I forgot about Milton's gift that day, and the next day when I inquired I was told that the guard with the large round head had taken ill. No sign of my package. But that first day was not a total loss. I had found the work by Candler that resonated with my deepest intuitions. By the time I returned home three months later, Milton Kasma was dead. The mystery of the gift went with him.

3.

Of the four hundred and twelve seats available in the reading room, I chose, day after day, the seat numbered B4. Why I chose that seat among so many others is a question to which I hold no answer. The "fact" of B4 was something ineffable, apparently utterly random, and yet a stroke of absolute coincidence, when one considers the web of life that one moves through, choosing strands this way and that, never quite sure where it will lead.

The same can be said of the Candler book, the one whose existence I had suspected. There were many books by and about this enigma, Edmund Candler, but only one book in which he exposed himself fully, only one book in which one could hear the singing of his blood from its deepest circuits.

Without much trouble, I found it, Candler's private journal, the dispatches never sent. I held it in my hand. Weighed it. There *is* something about a book. The way it allows the reader entry into the author's aloneness. The way it is expressed through this lonely act on the part of the writer...and the reader too, as if they were lovers at a distance, sharing what is most intimate — their aloneness.

On the first page, Candler spoke of the expedition in terms of an unveiling. Of course, he meant the unveiling of Tibet, of the ghostly city, Lhasa. Younghusband's expedition exposed that strange mountain civilization to the world, and exposed the world to it. I soon learned, however, that Candler's intentions went deeper. He wanted to unveil himself, he wanted to strip himself and his own civilization of any covering, any skin, so one could see the patterns of veins and arteries, the linking of bones, the energy that emanated when the body of the West made love with the body of the East.

From seat B4 I gazed up at the bell of the great dome, still weighing the book in my hand. The curved ceiling dropped to a frieze of windows brilliant with marching light, beneath which curved walls of reference volumes, thirty thousand of them more or less, and beyond them, ten million more books in this building and others, on one hundred and ten miles of shelving. All those books, and I had this one in my hand. An ordinary book, to be sure. Ordinary, but at the same time, magic. Common as the daily news, or the *Daily Mail*, or the grass, or the sun burning in its blue heaven.

The shape of the reading room continued to intrigue me — the way the readers' seats fanned out along the spokes of a wheel whose centre was composed of three rings housing the volumes of the catalogue. At the very heart of this wheel was a wicket where a young man, his spectacles resting on his nose and his short hair sticking straight up, had taken my application slips. An hour later, another young man, looking strangely similar to the first, had delivered the requested books to my place at B4.

I often wondered if the fellow at the centre ever felt the great weight of that responsibility on his shoulders. There at the heart of a wheel whose communication was, for the most part, silent and deep within the mind, he had to play the part of an active fulcrum, the gate-keeper, the Saint Peter of the British Library, so to speak. All in all, though, I suppose he considered it quite an ordinary job, not at all like searching for Irish bombs. And, in the end, it was probably for the best, or he might have started to consider himself the centre of a certain kind of universe and might have compared himself, in the most neurotic bothersome way, to Hitler or the Pope.

4.

Thus it was, day after day, reading of my great-great-uncle's journey into snow. Round about noon I would hear the tolling of distant bells from some London church, no doubt clinging with all its ancient might to the traditional way of time and I would, for a passing moment, delight in a certain sentiment, a wistful longing for the past and the peace of those days. This reverie would be immediately superceded by hunger and I would be off to the cafeteria for steak and kidney pie and a can of Newcastle Brown Ale, passing the Rosetta Stone on my way through the museum, as if it were nothing more than a fire hydrant or a post box.

After lunch there would be, perhaps, a film in the museum's cinema, something on Japanese kites or the carving of Tibetan thigh-bone horns, something colourful, hopefully, and then it was back to the reading room, back to B4, back to the book and Uncle Edmund's prose mountains.

After a week of this, I decided to pay a visit to the oldest living relative in my family, on the Candler side. Actually, her precise relationship to me has never been clear. Somewhere along the line, the Candler family tree, no doubt, lost a few branches in high winds, or was struck by lightning or suffered a season of amnesia-inducing drought. At any rate, she must have been a cousin of some sort, although in my family, she was always known as "Auntie."

5.

"Nineteen ought four," I corrected.

Auntie glared at me with the kind of dry maliciousness only a spinster of eighty long years can muster. "You're a smart aleck just like your father." She sipped her sherry, her long, once-patrician hands now all knuckles and knobby fingernails.

"As I was saying," she continued, "your great-great-uncle, my grandfather, entered Tibet in nineteen-ought...four" — she bowed in my direction — "and had many enough adventures to turn him into a queer old duck for the rest of his life."

"How so? What do you mean?"

"Well, of course, I only knew him when I was a child, but the thing that most intrigued me was that empty sleeve — you know he lost a hand in Tibet — had it shot off in some frightful mêlée with the natives. Now I can't recall whether it was the right or the left..." She put her hand to her chin, gazed out the window and fell into a silence, the silence of the old and unhurried.

"Yes, I've read about that," I added, not wanting to say more, afraid of altering the delicate reverie she had entered.

The sitting room in the house on Chesterton Row was cramped, chock to the brim with inherited ancestral Victorian furniture emanating age and weight, displays of china plates painted with Wordsworthian scenes, a silver tea set on a glittering tray and a rather maudlin, almost colourless budgie in a cylindrical cage.

I remember thinking it was the colour of dust and was quite likely the oldest budgie on record.

Auntie Liz was the last in a certain kind of familial line. It was as if all the objects assembled by a family over three or four generations had somehow found their way to this room where Auntie Liz was the zoo-keeper of this hoary menagerie.

"I remember how he used to gaze into the fire in his sitting room for hours on end." She spoke softly and seemed almost to be speaking to herself. "As if he were actually seeing something there. I asked him once, in my child's way, what it was he was looking at? He turned and smiled at me, he had the most wonderfully kind smile, and said, 'Why, the flames, of course, Elizabeth, the flames.' He patted me on top of the head, I must have been about seven years old then, and I can remember the most distinct feeling of heat on my skull, right through my hair.

"My parents didn't know what to make of him. Thought he was crazy as a loon. And yet I think they admired him in a way. Isn't that strange?" Turning in her chair, she pointed to a tall grandfather clock standing at the end of the room. "That was his, that clock. Hasn't worked for years. I should have it looked at, but I suppose it's too late now."

"What was his wife like?" I asked.

"Oh, a lovely woman. Very dignified and gentle. I remember her taking tea up to his study where he did his writing. After a while, he stopped writing for the newspaper, but he kept on writing something, I don't know what. Every time I came to their house,

13

he would either be in his study writing or in the sitting room watching the fire. I think they led a very simple, gracious life."

She turned to me then and inquired: "Would you like some Spotted Dick?"

A kind of pudding, I soon learned.

She carried in the little bowls herself on a metal tray that celebrated the coronation of Queen Elizabeth. We sat eating together, I with my legs crossed at the ankles, she in her large stuffed chair. She noticed me gazing about at the bric-à-brac.

"I've got something else of his, you know," she said, leaning forward as if conspiring. "Would you like to see it?"

She led me to a case with glass doors. Opening one with a key which caused her much distress in the finding, she pointed at a green stone statue of a Buddha about the size of a fist. "I told you he was a queer duck," she concluded, closing and carefully relocking the case.

The next day, sitting once again at seat B4 in the reading room of the British Museum, I thought about the statue. A simple stone carving, the sitting Buddha held one hand open at chest level, palm facing out. The other hand had been broken off.

6.

At the back of Candler's journal, there was a fold-out map to illustrate the route of Younghusband's expedition to Lhasa, the forbidden city, forbidden, that is, to foreigners, outsiders, the unknown world which would never understand its strange chants, its suspicions, its religious intrigues. The route was shown by a red line that slashed up and across the page from lower left to upper right, like the bold diagonal one finds in many paintings, the angle of energy.

In this case, the red line started at Siliguri in northern Bengal and ended at Lhasa on the edge of the vast Tibetan plateau. On the way, it passed through extreme western Bhutan and entered Tibet from the south, thrusting like a bolt of lightning up into higher and higher mountains. Dozens of towns and villages were linked by the snaking vein, including Gangtok, Chumbi and Gyantse.

It struck me, as I sat gazing at the map folded open on the desk at B4, that the bolt of lightning could just as easily have been seen coming out of Lhasa thrusting down into Bengal.

I recalled seeing a photograph of Candler that my maternal grandfather kept on the mantle. As far as I know, it was the only photograph of him that existed. It had been taken at Lhasa as he sat with four officers in front of the Mounted Infantry mess. In the distance, I noted a mountain saddle dipping between two peaks.

Closer by, a few peaked tents imitated the mountains. Directly behind the five, an enormous cluster of wildflowers in a bucket set on a table decorated the entrance to an open tent whose interior was the colour of black one finds only in old photographs, a black without relief, the black of lost time.

Three of the men sat on chairs, although Candler, at the far right, sat on a stool and leaned forward. Two other men sat on the ground in front: Lieutenant Rybot, the expedition's artist, on the left and Lieutenant Bailey, the expedition's photographer, on the right. Bailey held a puppy in his lap.

Across Candler's face slanted a shadow, leaving it half in light. His nose was large and wide; he had a widow's peak.

The photograph too was crossed by a bold diagonal, upper left to lower right. It began with the line of the tent, which wanted to float up and out of the picture, and ended with a peg stuck in the ground to which the tent flap was tied. The diagonal rope holding the tent down to the earth cut through Candler's upper torso. The photo was divided in two, Candler and the mountains on one side separated from the four men and the tent on the other.

Leaning back in my chair, I stared up at the dome and sighed. It was a coincidence, of course, Candler's separation from the others in the photo. A coincidence of a kind inescapable and true.

7.

Under the great dome of the reading room, I opened Candler's journal and read:

December 15, 1903   Chumbi   10,060 feet
Early today I wrote a dispatch which I must not send. I would be recalled in a moment and that must not happen. This strange land affects me in ways I cannot yet imagine. I feel raw, as if I am shedding a layer of skin, as if my heart at any moment will burst from my chest and release me into the rare cold air. It is not merely the height. I have been in mountains before. Something else, something else is moving within me. Yesterday we crossed the Ammo Chu and now I can see in the distance a great mountain the people here call Chumilari. My reports to the *Daily Mail* are mundane, filled with the details of troop movements and the progress of the expedition, but my feelings about the true expedition cannot be reported. No one would believe me. I have been through many strange lands, crossed the Gobi Desert by camel, slept half-frozen in high mountains of Central Asia, travelled with nomads who eventually tried to murder me, but here, here, there is something else, something unworldly, as if we are actually floating, yes floating miles above the earth.

And something else: throughout the entire affair there runs a strange but quite precise feeling of emptiness, as if the whole episode were constructed of air: soldiers of air marching into mountains of air, drawing maps of air, keeping records of air, for the attainment of an objective that is completely lacking in shape or substance.

This feeling of emptiness pervades all aspects of the expedition. The Tibetans themselves, for example. It turns out to be almost impossible to make any adjectives stick to them — as if the words were flakes of snow that melted as soon as they landed on their yak-skin coats. The people can barely be distinguished from the background of stone, yaks, donkeys, fields of barley, stunted brush, mountains hurtling up and down, loose rocks, moon, sun and cold clear light. I have seen turquoise lakes, and men and women with eyes of that colour. Their connection to the earth and sky and other elements is so basic, so genuine, so utterly manifest, that those elements can still be distinguished in their bodies and their speech. It seems they have risen out of the clay and walked, that all the aspects that combine coincidentally to make human life can still be seen in their faces — and all those aspects and elements are held together by that same emptiness that can also be distinguished in their faces.

Not the emptiness of depression, however. It is the emptiness of a mouth set in an O and about to speak, the circle of the sun spewing light...the void with its eyes open...

Recalling a line I had read the day before from near the end of Candler's journal, I took a sheet of paper and copied what he had written on first entering the forbidden city of Lhasa, after so much struggle, after terrorizing confrontations with life and death, after pain and heart-stopping delight at the beauty of the mountains: "Now that I am here in Lhasa, it is as if I am nowhere."

Gazing at the words, I let them dissolve into space until there was nothing left but sounds without meaning and, eventually, even the sounds faded into the silence between them...and then they returned. Picking the two essential words from the phrase, I wrote:

Now / here

Nowhere

CHAPTER II

1.

Boredom of waiting, for the sand to fall, for the stars to turn, for the journey to ratchet a notch forward. You could draw your finger across a map and the journey's done, but Candler experienced excruciating boredom in Tibet.

Boredom, the essence of life. All the important things happen in attendance on boredom. Waiting. We dream. We search for ways to fill the void.

Hot boredom gives way to hot excitement. The one bouncing to the other and back again. But cool boredom eases into cool excitement and they eventually become indistinguishable one from the other.

No more bouncing back and forth between the dream of arrival and where we are. There is only this place...and then a new place...and another.

Tuna was the name of a village where Candler spent the better part of a winter in Tibet, on a wide plain swept by bitter winds, a few scattered huts. A whole winter — nothing to do but eat yak brain and minal pheasant and wait.

Edmund Candler steps from his tent for a breath of fresh air. He has just finished dinner. The distant line of snow-browed mountains floats like clouds. For the first time in many days, his mind is empty of the contagion of thoughts that crowd in one upon the next. His mind, like a piece of ice, begins to melt. The sky a deep refreshing blue.

2.

Candler thought he saw something in the tree. A blue man, sitting, smiling ironically, his hair black, the shadows and light shifting. He squinted, trying to focus in the uncanny light. It was only the sky coming through the tightly woven branches. Or was it?

Time too shifted strangely. It seemed as if it had happened but a minute ago. Look again and it felt like years.

He recalled riding into Tibet on a pony he had bought in Darjeeling for three hundred rupees. Attempting to beat the other correspondent, Henry Newman, the one from Reuters, to the town of Chumbi. The usual eight-day trip Candler would cut to two. He was propelled by ambition, this one. The *Daily Mail* would be proud ... would shower him with praise. The pony panted as it climbed.

In the rhododendron zone, a strange thought struck him: What's the point of all this hurrying? Hurtling towards your end, each step a step closer to death, as if anything you do could have any meaning in the midst of this vast emptiness. He recalled earlier asking three charcoal burners the way: they stared at him as if he weren't human, as if he were a god or demon. But their eyes were not filled with fear — rather, a kind of shimmering blankness. Their empty gaze drifted again before his eyes.

The atmosphere was playing tricks on him. The stunted landscape, haunting contortion of limbs frozen in place: the stilling of all that furious and difficult growth terrified him.

The pony stumbled on a stone and Candler almost fell off. Ghosts that the pony's breath was making in the air would appear for a moment and then dissipate. The vague uneasiness clung to Candler. He stopped. Turning around in his saddle, he gazed back, wondering if he should return the way he had come.

Suddenly, down from the mountains came a wind that was cool and startling — startling because it seemed alive and seductive. Turning again, he rode on hard.

3.

I sit on the edge of the bed, having just woken from a dream. My eyes are still closed, I am only half here, drifting in and out of the silence as if my body is in several places at once, several times...

Candler's pony scurries up a mountain path nearing Tibet, loose stones slipping over each other, a mountain stream racketing down nearby. His journey is not separate from the lateness of the hour, here in London, the creaking of a nearby tree, the night wind in October leaves. He is always on his way up the mountain. Once a thing happens it happens repeatedly, forever, or how could it happen at all? The wind in those leaves, layered leaves, layered like the stones on a mountain path, layered like time, Candler and his pony passing through the leaves tonight.

But it never happened, none of it. Candler and his pony are a late-night dream, a windy dream in starless, cloud-bound skies. Nothing happened. No Candler, no mountain, no Tibet. These are words, images, memories formed of merest dust, rare as Everest air, empty of import, meaning or suggestion, impossible elucidations.

Thus it was the diaphanous clouds of breath from Candler's pony drifted up to join clouds over this city, clouds passing in our dreams, clouds passing in the windows of the city's towers. And a man constructed of words riding a pony constructed of words entered a land full of word mountains. Tibet.

4.

My thoughts turn back to Milton Kasma, the old Jew — not old really but all Jewish intellectuals have that aura of something fading away. Milton the waning moon. I want to fix his memory in my mind, discover who he was. But, of course, that is impossible, for he kept changing, like all of us.

Milton was always going away. I retain a stronger memory of the back of his head than his face. Even that day in Mirabel Airport — he left before I did. I sat waiting in the lobby, our last farewell echoing in the hall, and watched him leave, in his desultory way, just drifting off, not sure of the direction back. In fact, the first exit door he tried was locked and he had to use another. It seemed appropriate.

I recall sitting in the great domed hall of the reading room of the British Library the day a grey pigeon had found its way into the interior. It searched and searched, ultimately and only with the greatest difficulty finding the same crack by which it had entered, the sky waiting.

Already, Milton's face refused to resolve itself in my mind. He possessed all the details — don't get me wrong. He had eyes, eyebrows, lips and teeth in full measure and, if my memory serves me well, a nose in more than full measure. And hair, yes, he had hair, and not on the side of his head but on the top where it's supposed to be. He was, in all respects, normal, perhaps even super-normal. Except for one extraordinary feature — no one could ever recall what he looked like. It was uncanny. I would bump into Milton on a busy downtown street and almost not recognize him. He was always changing. His skin colour would appear slightly more olive or perhaps a touch more pale, his lips would be thicker or thinner, his head longer, shoulders more stooped.

Milton played on this characteristic, nurtured it. He would change his hairstyle from week to week, parting it first on the left side, then on the right, in the middle, and so on. One time he combed it all forward; another, straight back. He was not so much a chameleon as the kind of person who had embraced thoroughly the truth of impermanence and had decided to flaunt it.

Even his eyes were different. In the middle of a conversation, you would glance at him and notice that one eye was buoyant, the other withdrawn, or one eye laughing, the other red with fever.

His ears were enormous, that I recall quite clearly. And he once showed up at the movies with a nasty scar on his forehead which he insisted he had borne since the age of five. I had never noticed it before. Spending time with Milton could cause seasickness, you were always on shifting ground.

Few of my friends and none of my lovers could stand him. Either he talked incessantly or was morose and withdrawn, refusing to admit the existence of fellow human beings and refusing to conduct himself by the standards of normal social intercourse. On the other hand, he had the ability to address total strangers as if they were his intimates.

You never could tell the stranger who would listen, intrigued, and perhaps even reply, from that other kind of person who would hurry away from Milton, screaming inwardly. I never could tell, beforehand, how a person would react. I was never sure how I myself would react from one time to the next.

Did I start out by saying Milton Kasma was normal? All that I have described here is mere embellishment on that fading-away quality which was the empty core of what Milton was and where he was going.

Near the end, Milton said he had been rediscovering his Judaic roots — studying the Torah and the Kabbala, constructing complex charts, searching further and further back through the materialism of the modern age, into Protestantism and Christianity, into Judaism, its development and earliest history, back into shamanism and the ecstatic religions that engaged the earliest humans.

As always, Milton studied the subjects with an obsessive earnestness and a discipline so rigorous and thorough that, when he himself finally faded away, it seemed as if all those traditions, those beliefs and those thousands of years of philosophical grappling with the ultimate truths faded away with him. Suddenly they all seemed like embellishments. Milton had entered prehistory.

5.

January 8, 1904   Tuna

No schema, no preordained plan, is possible for us any more. We have entered prehistory, or perhaps we have gone beyond history. Or have we joined the two together? Breaking new ground, entering virgin mountains. Each step a step in a new direction. Maps have lost meaning...the ways arise to meet us...we must lose ourselves in the mountains, we must lose ourselves in the turquoise of lakes, we must be blinded by pure snows.

The dark grows darker and deeper, like mountain valleys, while the light grows unbearably bright in the rare air of icy peaks.

6.

Candler noted that as his journey progressed more deeply into Tibet, the villages and the people inhabiting them appeared more and more primitive. England seemed an imaginary place on the other side of the earth. Even Simla, the cool colonial capital of British India, with its gaming fields and racquet courts looked down upon by chattering monkeys in deodar trees and its circlet of snow-capped mountains, felt like the height of civilization compared to the raw, half-capsized villages that dotted the Tibetan route to Lhasa.

Not that the structures in those villages had the grandeur of great age — in fact, even recently constructed buildings gave the impression that they were on the verge of crumbling. Falling stones from houses and walls were a real danger to the troops.

As Tibet was penetrated, it was as if the expedition too had entered an earlier age. One village after another was more cut off from the outside world, more foul, the bodies of dead dogs were left in the streets to rot and be feasted upon there by rats, the callous vultures or other dogs. Each village felt more deserted than the last, even if occupied by a good-sized population. People stayed indoors as much as possible, squinting in their charcoal-blackened dens, sipping cup after cup of greasy buttered tea. A terrible stench pervaded everywhere, inside and out, from those half-decayed corpses of dogs littering the sewer channel in the middle of the streets. In some places, offal and refuse reached above the knees. The mouths and eyes of children ran with sores and ulcers. The faces and clothing of the adults were black from the ceaseless smoke, while the actual walls of the buildings were dark with grease. And at the end of a narrow street, the snows of a mountain could be seen striking a mile high into pure air.

Once Candler was invited into the hovel of the headman of one of these villages near where the expedition had encamped for a week to let the supply line catch up.

He was handed a cup of strong-smelling tea in what appeared to be a piece of skull-bone and was motioned to a spot near the low, crude stove. The air was stifling, the heavy oily smell suffocating. Candler steeled himself, not wanting to offend the headman, his wife, his two grown sons nor the wizened grandmother. Cautiously, a sip of tea passed his lips. He waited for some conversation to begin. Nothing happened. The others variously sipped their tea, stoked the fire or scratched themselves. No one said anything, nor was there any attempt to communicate.

At first, Candler was offended. They're making a fool of me, he thought. But then he looked more closely at them through the veiled gloom. No...no...I believe I am wrong...they mean no offence...this is just the way they are. He gazed at the old woman who felt his stare but was not shaken from her calm. She continued, her head bowed slightly, sitting in the dirt, doing...doing...nothing. Then something struck Candler with a force that almost knocked the cup from

his hand: These people are not only not talking —
they aren't thinking either! It was as if he suddenly
woke up. He looked at all of them, one by one. They
aren't thinking! he shouted inwardly, they aren't
thinking of anything! In that claustrophobic, murky
room, he caught the eyes of the grandmother, clear
and empty. Suddenly a vast space opened up, the space
of the mountains and the sky, which struck him like
a cold wind. Then the headman leaned forward, took
the cup from his hand and motioned for him to leave.

7.

Candler stretched out on the cot in his tent without
taking off his boots. Putting his hands behind his head,
he leaned back and gazed up blankly. I have been in
many strange places in the world, he thought, mountains almost as high as these, empty deserts, villages
lost from time, but this place gives me a feeling I've
never felt before. What is it? What is it? I'm at the
edge of something, about to fall, no, already falling,
it feels groundless, or backward, as if I had ridden
my pony backwards up the mountains. How strange,
how strange, he mumbled as he drifted off to an uneasy
sleep, discordant images flickering behind his eyelids:

the face of the old Tibetan grandmother, empty though kind, an iron wheel turning backwards, flakes of snow melting on the backs of his hands.

8.

General J.R.L. Macdonald, CB, of the Royal Engineers, the commander of the Tibet Mission Escort, was bald on the top of his head with a fringe of hair around the edges. A lustrous, bountiful moustache spread in a wide upside-down V beneath his straight nose. His high forehead was accentuated by the baldness. He had the square jaw and severity of a Scotsman, which he was, and he appeared to have an extra fold of skin on his eyelids, lending his dark unsettled eyes a rather discomfitting look. In China during the Boxer Rebellion three years earlier, he had been the Director of Balloons.

"I shall not have it!" he was explaining rather too forcefully to Colonel Younghusband, the civilian commander of the expedition. "The man cannot even brew a decent pot of tea. I shall take one of the Gurkhas as my servant — and you can send this native back to wherever it is he came from."

Younghusband could see it was no use arguing. He sighed, his soft, troubled eyes looking out through the flaps in the tent towards the massing of light and the distant mountains. Why was Macdonald always most vehement about the things that did not matter? When it came to the real questions, about the expedition, supplies, health of men and animals and so on, he was hedging, indecisive, useless. But this — tea!

"Perhaps someone else here can make use of the man," Younghusband said, surveying the others seated on rough camp chairs in the large tent, assembled for the weekly operations meeting.

Candler looked at the others. Major Iggulden, Macdonald's Chief of Staff; J.C. White, with fourteen years' experience on the Tibetan frontier; Major Fred O'Connor, a gunner who spoke Tibetan; Mr. Hayden, the Mission geologist; Captain Walton, the medical officer; the red-headed, flamboyant Ottley of the Mounted Infantry; Henry Newman, the Reuters correspondent and an old friend of General Macdonald's; Lieutenant Rybot, the expedition's official artist, with a pad in his hand; Lieutenant Bailey, the official photographer, a lover of animals; and finally, Mitter, Younghusband's Parsi clerk.

No one spoke up so Candler said, "I can use him," and that was that.

"What's his name?" Candler asked General Macdonald as they were leaving the tent later.

"Unpronounceable...I called him Sarge, after an American soldier who fought with us in China. The native bears a slight resemblance to him," the Colonel answered curtly, and walked away briskly to his quarters.

9.

Sarge had been captured in an insignificant skirmish early in the expedition. He had then agreed to become an officer's servant rather than spend the long winter trying to return to his home in Kham, a region in far-off eastern Tibet. Though stocky, he was Candler's height, the men of Kham being the tallest in the country. The Tibetan stood before the correspondent in his skirt-like *chuba* and high, soft leather boots. They looked at each other.

That first look was important. It was empty of any preconceptions until Candler thought: Will he slit my throat while I sleep? The man stared at him with a look that was impossible to gauge. Candler could have read anything into it. If Candler thought, Friendly, the man looks friendly, then the fellow would appear friendly. If Candler thought, He's an idiot, incapable of any skill, the man would look like an idiot. And so on. Sarge was still staring at him, seemingly blank, open, saying nothing.

Apparently the man had learned English from Major O'Connor with astounding rapidity.

"Sarge, you are my servant now. Do you understand?"

Sarge bowed his head, at one with his fate, but not grovelling. There was an inescapable pride in his demeanour, the way he held his head, his composed face. "Happy to leave General Macdonald," he announced, "not a good man."

The winter spent awaiting orders to move out for Lhasa was endlessly boring. Holed up for months near Chumbi and Tuna, Candler and Sarge spent their time taking long walks through nearby villages, across deserted, snow-scattered fields, into the foothills. Candler was learning Tibetan while Sarge was improving his English. At least that was the outer form of their discussions. The content of these forays into language was something else, something that was certainly not gratuitous, but followed a pattern and order that seemed to be sneaking up on Candler. And always, at the very heart of their conversations, was the silence of the mountains, so close, yet untouchable.

10.

Candler and Sarge had been talking about the total numbers of Younghusband's expeditionary force. Four companies of the 23rd Pioneers, a machine-gun section of the Norfolk Regiment, twenty Madras sappers and others. Twenty-five hundred men in all, and at least twice that many coolies for carrying supplies. Down in the valley, they could see tents set up near the river, which was showing a single pulse of open water in the brisk mid-winter afternoon. Evening was coming quickly and a sliver of moon took to the indigo sky.

No clouds. They just stood together looking at it, the unusually clear moon, without saying a word.

Candler was struck with the unutterable beauty of the place. A few towering spruce trees commanded the near distance, their foliage like umbrellas over the valley. Rags of mist strayed beneath the peaks of the closest mountains. The line of the frozen river could be discerned threading the valley like a ribbon of white silk. A peace he had never before felt descended on him. He thought he might never leave this place, and he sensed a close kinship with the land, and especially with the man standing next to him. There was no explanation for it, why he was there, why he felt so buoyant and joyful. Sighing, he decided for the moment not to attempt to figure it out. Sarge touched his shoulder and they began to descend, heading back to camp. Evening circled in like a round, blue tent of silk.

11.

January 22, 1904   Dochen

We haven't a clue where we're going. Deeper into the mystery of Tibet which keeps turning out, on closer inspection, to be no mystery at all, but the most ordinary of ordinaries.

Perhaps one could look at it this way: from a distance the mountains appear silver and white, glowing, with an impression of unfathomable vastness. Once you were actually in them, however, they were brown, dull, only a portion of what you had imagined them to be.

That's it — imagination! What you dream never quite materializes. This strange, empty land with its mountains, silver, mysterious, vast presences, exists only in your mind. Once you touch the mountain, it becomes a paltry handful of pebbles and dirt. But wait — look at it. You hold the mountains in your hand!

12.

It was not the best way to spend a Tibetan winter, in a "den," a hole dug in the ground, walled up with boulders and roofed in with green fir branches, but it was adequate and certainly better than the wind-torn tents issued to the soldiers.

A pine fire crackled and spat sparks, pumping a pleasant warmth into the room. Candler had just finished a meal of minal pheasant and yak's heart (again) and was leaning over a medic's operating table which served as his desk. As he wrote, he listened to a gramophone scratching sweetly in the corner:

Her golden hair was hanging down her back...

He was humming along, involved in his work, when a distant, other-worldly wail raised the hairs on the back of his neck, sending a chill up his spine. Suddenly the fire seemed like a pitiful defence against the night, a laughable security. Standing up, he walked to the gramophone and turned up the volume. He could hear the bitter wind as particles of snow drifted into the *den*. Candler cranked the music up higher but could not drown out the wind or the animal wail which came again.

Her golden hair... her golden hair... her...

The gramophone needle was stuck, doomed to repeat again and again its mindless refrain. Touching the arm, he saw the needle slip across the record with a screeching sound, bringing an unwanted, uncomfortable silence.

Walking to the door, Candler folded back the heavy blanket and the outer canvas. There was no moon. Never had he seen such a black pitiless night. It seemed to overwhelm the light from his lamp. The mountains were invisible, the stars blotted out by a thick muffle of cloud. Even the nearest tent was gone, impossible to discern, as if it had been swallowed up by a crack in the earth.

With a shock, he realized Sarge was standing in front of him. Candler stumbled backwards, unable to suppress a frightened whimper. Sarge stood at the door looking in, while Candler quickly regained his composure. "You frightened me," he tried to explain.

"Death is near. Stay in house," Sarge announced and turned away.

Candler thought it was odd the way it was said. There was no doubt it was an order, coming from a voice practised at authority. Candler also realized it was said for his own good.

13.

January 29, 1904   Chalu

The land of snow. Ice-brilliant, indifferent, refreshing snow. Mountains piled high with it, valleys deep with it. Thousands of miles of snow, every pore of it emitting light. Flushed pink at dawn when sunlight curls around the mountain's edge, or glowing gold at dusk. Blinding at midday or casting deep blue shadows by mid-afternoon. Snow pure and unadulterated, primary snow, before man or thought of man, untouched, absolute.

Leaning back in my chair at B4, I thought about snow. Books and books of it. Coming at you in storms, or falling gently, but somehow managing to cover every corner, every crevice, every question. Or compressing into immovable density over a long, burdensome winter, for thousands of pages, falling day after day, filling up every page from beginning to end, top to bottom, snow letters, snow words, snow lines piling up.

Then you try to hold it in your hand and it changes, slips away. Because it won't be held, too wild, too pure a thing for that, like a butterfly, the monarch, its sparkling dust of pigment coming off on your hands.

Falling snow covers up all tracks, all traces, all memories, like time itself, making a tale of memory a race against time, trying to catch the outlines of the earth, splayed paths, tracks of animals before they are obliterated forever, before spring comes again, taking with it the memories and the lost memories and giving birth once again to the new time.

I looked at the walls around me and suddenly felt I was being buried alive by books, walled in as in Poe's tale, the letters, words, lines, pages, books, collections and volumes of books cutting me off from the world and the crisp, almost painful wind I needed to wake me up. I resolved to visit Auntie Liz once again.

14.

"He didn't put it in books," she said, a few days later, as we sat on a bench in the chill November air in Hyde Park. "He told me the whole tale but it is not the one he wrote down. In fact, he couldn't write it down," she added, her rheumy eyes watching some distant children at play.

I was seeing a side of Auntie Liz I had never before seen. She seemed unconscious that she was revealing a part of herself that was not the little old lady I had known. She had taken on an air of mystery, of being beyond time, and it made all her other attributes seem like the accoutrements of a player, an actor. Wanting to see more, and longing to unlock her knowledge of Candler, I persisted.

"Why not?" I asked, hoping that her direct contact with Candler would somehow clear up the question that had been plaguing me. "Why can't I find out exactly what happened there to Candler?"

"Because, young man, when you write it down it runs away. You must experience it. It's like death... you can read all you want to about it, you can look at dead people and try to imagine it, but there is only one way to find out the truth about it... and that is to die."

I nodded and glanced at dark clouds over the city. They were threatening snow. I wondered why the questions would not clarify themselves — perhaps if I could clearly define them, they would open up and release me.

"It's as easy as sticking a key in a door," she added. "Once you're through, you don't hold on to the key. Or the door handle. You walk through."

I nodded. "Let's walk," she said.

As we walked along, I tried to pinpoint in my own mind what it was that Candler had learned in Tibet, what had happened to him that had changed everything, and why it was so difficult to translate into words. Then it struck me — I could imagine Candler walking along a mountain path in Tibet, struggling with the same questions.

Having stopped to gaze up at the heavy clouds for a moment, trying to sort out these thoughts, I noticed Auntie Liz had continued walking. I turned and followed in her footsteps, pleased momentarily by the regular tapping of her cane.

15.

Ahead of him, walking through the snow (Candler could feel the sadness coming off the other's back), Sarge stopped, turned: "Why have you English come here?"

Candler mouthed the only explanation he had heard: "Because of the Russians and because we wish to trade with you."

"We have nothing, we want nothing," he retorted, his arms spread wide as if taking in all the empty land around. "And I have seen no Russians in Lhasa or anywhere else in Tibet."

"The Viceroy of India, Lord Curzon," Candler insisted, "believes there are Russians in Tibet. Colonel Younghusband too believes there are Russians in Lhasa even now turning the Dalai Lama against the British. If Tibet goes to the Russians, all of India will be threatened."

Sarge turned, continued walking.

"You have heard of Dorjieff?" Candler asked.

"Yes, I know the Mongol." Sarge did not turn around but continued the seemingly aimless walk a short distance from the camp.

Candler followed. "Dorjieff is a Russian citizen, he has the Dalai Lama's ear. We have it on good authority that Dorjieff has been known to meet with the Tsar's assistant, a monk named Rasputin. This Rasputin has much power over the Emperor of Russia. Have you not seen the Russian soldiers in Lhasa?"

"No Russian soldiers in Lhasa." Sarge shook his head.

"They must be well hidden then."

"No Russian soldiers hidden in Lhasa."

His persistence annoyed Candler. How could he pretend to know so much, this servant from eastern Tibet? And yet the authority of his statements sounded absolutely unquestionable. It was different with him than with Younghusband or Macdonald or even with Lord Curzon, whom Candler had met at Simla the previous summer. Those men were racked with doubt; even as they insisted on their version of things in Tibet or anywhere else, one always felt that they were unsure of themselves, uncertain. Most of the time they could hide this uncertainty with consummate skill; on the surface they exhibited, especially in Curzon's case, a cold clarity. But the doubt sometimes slipped through in unguarded moments.

It struck Candler then that this uncertainty was a deep fear — one they were afraid to confront in themselves. A bottomless crevice that was horrifying because they knew one day they would fall through it, no matter what. Sarge was the only person he had ever met who stared at this crevice all the time, without flinching. It gave his bearing and his speech an authority that was uncanny, as if the words that he spoke had come up out of the earth and rang on the cold air. Candler believed him, and began to wonder what this expedition was really all about.

16.

Milton Kasma too had made a journey. A scholarly journey, into his roots, through his own personality, into something else. It was terrifying to realize how little hold he had on anything. But he wasn't crazy

— although he may have appeared so to some. Like the ladies in the shoe department at Eaton's.

One afternoon, I happened upon him sitting in one of the chairs at the edge of the shoe department. I sat down. One did not have to greet Milton in the normal way — he had passed beyond mere salutations.

He turned to me. "I love Muzak," he announced.

I nodded. "How long have you been sitting here, Milton?"

He checked his watch. It could have been a painting by Rembrandt for all the attention and delight he lavished on consulting it. "Two hours."

"Have you bought any shoes?"

He checked his feet. "I never buy ladies' shoes," he said, "they're all style, no content."

Every few moments, the salespeople would cast furtive glances at us, but no one approached.

"Oh, this is my favourite," Milton said, glancing up into the air as the Muzak changed tunes.

He mumbled along with the strings: "To everything, turn, turn, turn..."

I listened. "I've got to go, Milton," I said, starting to get up.

He put his hand on my arm. "Stay, please," he said, so I did, because he had said it with a familiar fervent desperation that always meant "I mean it, you might learn something."

Relaxing in the seat, I decided to play out this little game. I slipped into the music. Watched people pass. Smelled roasting nuts from two aisles over. Noticed a red sweater I liked. I listened to the music, balancing on it, floating with it, still hearing it even when I turned to Milton and whispered, "Milton, this is ridiculous!"

He nodded at something across the aisle in the travel section. It turned out to be a poster of snow-capped mountains. "I'm going there," he said, and then a white-haired saleslady asked us to leave.

"I really enjoy Muzak," he said to her as we were leaving. He was completely sincere. She smiled.

Later, we walked down Ste. Catherine Street. Stars were popping out, lights flashing on, late shoppers hurrying home.

"I still don't understand why you want to do this thing on Candler," Milton said. "Why not work on something closer to home, like St. Catherine, patron saint of taffy?"

"I don't know," I answered. "It's guesswork, really. But you pick up little cues that point out certain directions and you follow them. For example, a friend left a copy of one of Candler's books at my cabin in the country. Actually, I never learned who left it, I just supposed it was a friend."

"Do you remember in 'The Secret Sharer' when Conrad talks about the chief mate who found a scorpion drowned in the ink-well of his writing desk?" Milton was loping along at a good speed. "Watch out for words."

"Or develop a bold stroke," I punned.

Milton turned on me, his eyebrows knit together. "Sorry," I mumbled.

"What do you think of Mishima trying to bring together the life of art with the life of action?" Never did Milton feel the need to burden his speech with sequiturs and, I must admit, the sheer audacity and spontaneity that was the working of his mind intrigued me, no, not "intrigued," rather it kept me on a kind of edge, kept me on my toes ready for anything that might arise. When in this state, I could see things that I would not normally see, for example, the red stoplights reflected in long slim minimal lines in the brushed steel light-poles along the street.

"Mishima raised some interesting questions," I ventured.

"I think Mishima was a fool. It breaks my heart he was such a fool. What is the purity of discipline without a touch of warmth or compassion? Damn it!" Milton was waving his arms about, shouting, drawing stares from the late shoppers and early fun-seekers. He started to walk along the edge of the curb, balancing between sidewalk and street. "He wasn't a Samurai," Milton concluded, "no, not a Samurai of any sort."

We walked on in silence.

"So, it's Edmund Candler, is it?" Milton turned to me. "Another of the long-dead you hope to resuscitate. Don't you know it's impossible?"

"Why attempt the possible?" I posed.

He stopped in his tracks, smiled broadly, threw his arm around my shoulders and kissed me on the cheek.

CHAPTER III

————— • —————

1.

In a corner of the tent, Sarge sat on a cot, stared at the floor and smiled to himself.

Next to the rough table between Candler and Lieutenant Bailey stood Bailey's camera. As they talked, Candler noticed their reflection in the camera's lens and thought it was strange, how they appeared to be in another room in the distance, the camera drinking them in.

Bailey's tamed mallard sat in his lap, sleeping.

"The further I get from home," Candler continued, "the closer I get to home, if you know what I mean."

"No, actually, I don't know what you mean. Want some rum?" Bailey asked, lifting his eyebrows, reaching for the bottle on a nearby shelf.

"Rum? I haven't had rum since England. Nothing but gin in India — tiresome stuff."

"To the King!" Bailey raised his glass. They drank.

"What I mean is — here we are nearly on the roof of the world, London seems further and further away, and I never felt so close to understanding the people I know back there — my wife, my friends, my old self."

"I make no attempt to understand people," Bailey said, "only animals."

Bailey had wavy sand-coloured hair, broad shoulders, a ready smile. He did not seem to belong on this expedition of dyed-in-the-wool career men from Britain, sturdy hard-bitten Gurkhas from Kashmir and the handful of adventurers that made up the twenty-five hundred of the expeditionary force. In fact, now that Candler thought of it, it did not seem that he himself belonged here either, at least not with Macdonald, Younghusband and company. Of course, he wasn't a soldier, he was a journalist, so he was already separate in that sense. The only other journalist, Henry Newman, was an impossible prig who knew several of the higher ranking officers from their days together in China and spent most of his time with them. Candler realized that he himself sought out the eccentrics, but even with them, there was often a barrier that he couldn't define. When he tried to express what was going through his mind, they would look at him strangely. Bailey didn't understand him either, although at least he accepted him despite everything.

And yet there was something more, something he would not dare express to any except the easy-going Bailey. Every day he felt further from the group, as if they were living in some strange reality that was completely imagined, conjured up. It seemed that they were headed off towards some goal that had absolutely no meaning, that they could never justify the actions they took, as if once they had decided on Lhasa, there was nothing that could turn them back even though they all sensed there was absolutely nothing there.

"Sometimes I believe it is sheer bullheadedness driving us to Lhasa," he commented to Bailey.

"Truly, it's madness — this whole affair is madness. I heard Ottley the other day say that he will cut his way to Lhasa on his own if he must. The fools expect gold there. It's craziness. And what they are doing to the animals disgusts me. So many have died of anthrax, foot-and-mouth and rinderpest, it's terrible."

"Yes, the lower Tista Valley was hard on them, and us too. All that tropical heat, and then the climb and this cold. I hear a number have died from eating monkshood."

Bailey stroked the feathers on the back of the mallard's neck. "Macdonald has tried mules, bullocks, ponies, yaks, buffaloes. I heard a story last night — you know what he tried to do — it's maddening — he ordered up six camels. Camels! Can you believe

51

it! They all died before reaching Chumbi."

"Speaking of which — Macdonald himself is not looking well these past weeks. He's keeping to his bed much of the time."

"I have heard. Colonel Younghusband is furious," Bailey added. "They are not getting along."

"Strange — the closer we get to breaking camp and heading for Lhasa, the worse Macdonald gets, as if he's resisting it."

2.

Several days later, the force began the arduous trek towards Lhasa, where the Dalai Lama waited in his palace, impertinently refusing to answer the diplomatic letters sent him by Lord Curzon. That first day, Sarge and Candler rode side by side across a broad desolate valley, talking for hours. At last, Sarge pointed straight ahead, saying, "So you think you are going to Lhasa!" and laughed. "Show me Lhasa. Is it there?" he said. Then pointing back the way they had come, he said, "Is it there?" Pointing to the right: "There?" To the left: "There? Show me Lhasa. Or perhaps it is here, in this place, under our feet, over our heads. Where is Lhasa?" All that Candler could manage was a shrug. After that, they were silent, and Candler wondered what he meant and yet, in another way, understood.

Sitting back in my chair in the British Library, I thought about Candler and what that statement must have meant to him. It reminded me of Milton's theory of Troy.

Milton believed that the repetition of the *Iliad*, first orally and then written, but always in the imaginations of human beings for thousands of years, had actually created those battles between Hector and Achilles, had actually somehow imagined into existence the stone walls of Troy, the dramatic events, the layers of ruins discovered by Schliemann in the nineteenth century. Until then everyone thought that Troy was a myth, a city in a tale. Well, it was a city in a tale, Milton explained, but the tale had power and after a long period of time, the tale came to life. Milton pointed to the Tibetans' belief in certain "beings" as another example of this type. The Tibetans, he explained, believed in beings that had been created over thousands of years by the accumulated thoughts and emotions of real human beings. In other words, call it a ghost, call it a spirit, there was an actual being, a collection of energies, which embodied malevolence, and another which embodied delight, another of innocence, another of boredom, another of anger, passion, confusion, exertion and so on. There were also lesser beings that embodied the particular characteristics of a place.

"Time is a strange medium," he said. "Time is the key. We like to think there are three times but there is only one time. The future lives in the lines of force just beyond the tips of our fingers, the future lives in the constructions of the imagination. The past is still here happening over and over again. The Trojan Wars repeated themselves for so long in so many imaginations that stone and wood gathered into a city. Schliemann found the ruins that were left. The tale embodied itself. Of course, it was a powerful tale to begin with and could capture people's imaginations."

After this discussion with Milton, a kind of cloud of ambiguity rose up in my system, as if I had been inoculated with a different view of the world, one that was totally alien to me, but whose power was undeniable. It seemed as if I moved through an imaginative mist, the city around me, the formerly comfortable hill of Mont Royal topped by St. Joseph's Oratory, all appeared as utterly ephemeral, myself included. Luckily, Milton had pointed out that, though entirely ephemeral, the world still mattered.

It struck me that the world had been suddenly emptied, and then reappeared a moment later three feet to the left. Once I grew used to this idea, I knew I would find it considerably refreshing.

Thinking about these things at seat B4, I wondered how Candler felt once he realized the mountains and valleys of Tibet across which he was trudging were, in effect, clouds. His Western mind must have hovered at the edge of the abyss, the abyss which was its own essence.

3.

Macdonald stretched out on his back on the pallet which was being hefted by six Gurkhas. He stared at the clouds and puffed on a cigarette. Coughing, he leaned over and spat. The long narrow file of men, animals and wagons was led by Ottley and Younghusband on grey horses. Macdonald was about a third of the way back.

The line halted. Candler's pony went trotting past. "What's going on?" Macdonald asked, leaning up on his elbow, wanting to be in control yet lacking the energy to carry it through.

"It appears," Candler muttered as he gazed through his binoculars, "that we have met the Tibetan army."

"Good God," Macdonald uttered as he collapsed back onto the stretcher.

Candler continued riding to the front where Younghusband's troops had massed and gathered along a wall of loose stones, a sangar, that ran clear across a narrow point at the mouth of a valley. Noticing the sky was almost violet, Candler rode up near Younghusband and dismounted. On the far side of the three-foot high wall stood about seven hundred Tibetan soldiers in *chubas* and fur caps, some holding rifles which were absurdly out of date.

Younghusband and Ottley were speaking to the Tibetan general who stood on the far side of the wall. The general looked like a sturdy peasant and had fiery eyes which looked on the British with distaste and a certain amount of edgy, repressed anger. A difficult, tense conversation ensued, complicated by the need for translation by Major O'Connor, a short man with spectacles, standing to Younghusband's left.

As they discussed who would do what, Candler noticed Sarge approach the wall nearby. A Gurkha had surreptitiously raised his rifle and taken aim at the Tibetan general's heart. Slowly, Sarge raised his hand and placed it on top of the rifle, forcing it down. The Gurkha gave him a quizzical look but acquiesced.

The air was absolutely silent but for the strained conversation that was taking place. The Tibetans seemed fearful but resolute, hardly an army at all but a mass of undisciplined farmers and shepherds. At that moment, Candler thought he would take some notes on the discussion and the scene. Reaching back towards his pony to remove a notebook from his saddlebag, he heard a shot ring out. It was followed by a moment of uncanny silence — before an uproar of firing and shouting ensued and Candler realized his right hand had been blown to pieces by a quick, nervous shot from the Tibetan general himself. Within ten minutes, two hundred Tibetans lay dead or wounded in the field, the rest dispersed. Only five British had been felled, one fatally.

CHAPTER IV

———— • ————

1.

A month later Candler was back with the expeditionary forces in Tibet, his arm in a sling. "After several
weeks recovering in Darjeeling," he explained to Sarge,
"I decided to visit an old friend in Banaras. Strange
place, this city on the Ganges. One day, out for a
stroll, I walked down the steps to one of the ghats
at the edge of the water. A young Hindu fellow, in
the best Oxford English, requested my assistance to
help him place his father on the funeral pyre. There
didn't seem to be any other relatives about. Wrapped
in pure white cloth, the sheer weight of the dead body
amazed me. It had a weight that was not only physical,

but elemental, as if the fact of this death sank like a thought, with the gravity of a deep imponderable thought.

"He lit the twigs and the blaze roared forth. As it burned, we watched the river flowing by and said little. Something made me stay on and on until the flame exhausted itself and the ashes cooled. A bit of a breeze had come up and the son was terrified that his father's ashes would blow away before they could be scattered on the holy waters. Finally, he tossed them in the air where they drifted around for a while, refusing to come to their resting place, but at last they floated down and settled on the waters heading to the sea. This scene reminded me of a fire I saw once in my childhood village. The minister's house had caught fire. By the time help arrived, it was too late. We watched the house burn, fed by the thousands of books in the minister's library. He was known as the most learned man in the county. I remember seeing pages of text, ash, that is, no longer paper, floating up on the flames, over our heads and settling on the surrounding fields. I looked at some of them. You could still read the words, but if you touched them, they crumbled. They all disappeared the next day in a gentle rain." A grimace darkened Candler's face.

"It still pains you?" Sarge asked, nodding at the arm in the sling.

Candler nodded.

They heard someone approaching the tent. Ottley ducked in, tall, gaunt, eyes ablaze, red hair impeccably groomed. "Welcome back, Candler," he smiled, ignoring the presence of Sarge. "Might be a bit closer to a fair fight with these natives if we all fought with one hand."

Candler smiled, embarrassed by Ottley's attempts at bonhomie. "I hear the fighting has gone well since my absence."

"Gone well? My boy, the natives of this land don't know a rifle from a dowsing stick. The Russians must be supplyin' 'em with the most out-o'-date weapons they've got, but the bloody devils can't shoot anyway. Sometimes I'm ashamed to be whupping them."

"Then why do you do it?" Sarge spoke up with an air of authority so unexpected it sent both Candler and Ottley into a shocked silence. Ottley glared at Sarge with utter disbelief that one of the natives would have the gall to say anything to him, let alone question him as an equal.

Ottley refused to speak directly to Sarge. He turned to Candler. "Your manservant was gone much of the time you were in Darjeeling." He glared again at the Tibetan sitting quietly on a blanket on the floor. "There's some talk he's a spy. If I were you, Candler, I'd worry about getting my throat slit in the middle of the night."

Sarge, gazing at the floor, said, by way of explanation, "I was in a cave in the mountains, alone. I was praying, that is all."

Ottley, already bowing out the door-flap, harrumphed.

The two friends, for that is now what they had become, sat in silence. Then Sarge spoke. "The Tibetans do have ancient rifles but they are not such bad shots. You English will never understand. We do not want to kill you. If we could scare you away, that would be enough. We are Buddhists. We do not kill, men or beasts. The Tibetans have been shooting over the heads of the Gurkhas and the British. Of course, some of our young men do get angry, but for the most part we are very patient. You may think you are conquering us, but, like a subtle and powerful woman, we are overwhelming you simply by giving in." He looked up from the floor and smiled broadly at Candler.

2.

Sagarmatha. Chomo-lungma. Goddess Mother of the Snows. Everest. A mountain of many names. Sarge and Candler stood on a high mountain path gazing at Everest many miles away.

"What can one say," Candler mused, stunned by the view.

"The mountains are a mystery," Sarge observed, squeezing Candler's shoulder through his thick coat, "and within that mystery many other mysteries are hidden."

Candler thought of his wife for the first time in many weeks. Veronica was in London, waiting. Once a month, their letters passed on the high seas. It all seemed unreal.

The two friends heard a soft musical voice in the distance. Approaching along the path was a young woman driving a yak. Every few paces she would flick the animal with a polished stick she held in her hand, saying "Eeuk-eeuk" to the beast. Then she would return to the wordless song she was humming.

As she approached, Sarge greeted her and she stopped to chat, as if there were no war going on in the valley below. As she smiled, Candler noted her strong beauty in a wide face. She smelled faintly of juniper smoke.

As they spoke, Sarge ran his hand along the yak's spine, tugging at the thick, matted hair. The girl glanced at Candler's empty sleeve and giggled, saying something to Sarge about it. Sarge laughed and the girl offered Candler a piece of dried meat. As Candler chewed, she left, in no hurry to reach her destination.

"What did she say?" Candler asked.

"You don't want to know. Nothing important."

"Wasn't she afraid? Doesn't she know what's happening in the valley?"

"This one has no fear. She has never been to the valley. Perhaps it was the Mountain Goddess herself." Sarge turned towards Chomo-lungma.

"That's ridiculous, She was just a yak-herder, a flesh-and-blood woman," Candler insisted.

"Did you smell the smoke?" Sarge asked.

Candler nodded. He had an overwhelming desire to get back to the camp as soon as possible. This was all too strange.

"Yes, perhaps you are right, she was just a woman."

As they returned, they heard the sound of horns, a strange wail, echoing among the gorges and ravines at lower elevations.

"There is a monastery nearby," Sarge said, hurrying through fir trees and rhododendrons.

They soon found it, perched on an outcropping of rock overlooking a deep chasm at the bottom of which flowed a sinewy river. It appeared as if it had grown out of the rock itself, the way sugar or salt crystallizes along a spine of string.

The sound of the horns was so ancient and all-pervading that it seemed its ceasing would lead to the slow collapse of the jumbled brown cubes that were the walls of the monastery, as if the sound itself were their reason for existence. And if the walls collapsed, then the mountains themselves would soon be crumbling away. It was odd, Candler thought, in this place where all appeared hard, ancient and immovable, one was confronted constantly with a deep, overwhelming sense of groundlessness. Perhaps it was the heights, the thin air, the vast abysses, but everything felt topsy-turvy, like that monastery perched on its ledge, about to tumble into the ravine.

They entered the *gompa*, the interior, where an old, bald-headed monk in simple robes met them. Several young monks, boys of seven or eight years, stared at them from behind the robes of the elder monk. He and Sarge talked.

"He says that some British on horses were here early this afternoon. He says the leader had red hair," Sarge translated.

"It must have been Ottley with his men," remarked Candler.

"There are only old men and boys here now, so they did not stay. But the old man is very upset. He says the one with the red hair threatened to take one of the boys. This is very bad."

Candler thought it strange indeed that the old monk invited them to drink tea despite the actions of his compatriots. For months the British had been approaching the capital, fighting battles at every narrow valley and medium-sized town along the way, always with the same result — high casualties for the brave but disorganized Tibetans and another victory for the expedition. And yet, there was no smell of defeat among these people. They remained cheerful.

3.

April 8, 1904   Samando

Who is this Sarge, this rough Tibetan peasant who has taken over my life? I begin to wonder if the world has not turned upside down. Several days ago, we visited a monastery. On leaving the *gompa* and coming out to the cobbled courtyard, we once again saw a young woman we had seen on a high path earlier in the day, a yak-herder. She waited with several old monks near a pile of sticks heaped up as if for a bonfire. The air smelled like juniper. Strangely, it seemed as if they had been waiting for Sarge. He spoke to them, motioned towards me. Next they sat down, cross-legged, beside the heap. After a few moments, the woman started rubbing her hands together in the oddest way, sliding her hands back and forth, back and forth, as if enacting some kind of ritual. Then Sarge reached forth and took her hands in his, held them a moment, turned to the sticks and lit them. Immediately, the dry sticks blazed forth. But, there is this that makes my mind teeter at the edge: I saw nothing in his hands, nothing!

Sarge turned to me and smiled and the warmth of his smile calmed my fears. He told me to sit, which I did. We sat facing the fire, quite close to it. The heat was unbearable. As I tried to turn away, Sarge said, "Look at the fire. Do not turn away or you will die." I stayed, trusting him, knowing he spoke the truth. I could feel the hairs on my eyebrows curling, my skin raging. The others appeared unaffected. Within the fire I noticed a small Buddha melting. It must have been made out of butter or fat. The air was heavy with the scent of juniper, and the heat waves gave the scene an other-worldly air. For ten minutes we stayed thus. The fire quickly burned itself down to ashes and coals and then we stood. I was shaking as if with cold. My lips were burned and it hurt when I slid my tongue over them. My hair was full of ashes.

Sarge seemed proud. Then he spoke. "You British, you do not understand fire." It seemed uncanny to me. Why was he looking at the yak-herder when he said it, instead of at me to whom the words were spoken?

Then the woman rubbed a soothing potion on my face and hands and Sarge and I took our leave.

4.

Milton and I often talked about women. He said women were always coming in and out of his life. He said they didn't understand his needs and readily admitted that he didn't understand theirs either. For several years, in trying to comprehend his strained relations with women, he went through analysis and concluded: Next to Jung, Freud was a midget, a footnote in the history of the mind. When I asked him to elaborate, he refused, a most uncharacteristic response.

When asked to tell something about his childhood, however, Milton was never one to refuse or hesitate or even know when to stop. Because I had shown an interest once, long before, in his upbringing, Milton concluded that I was interested forevermore in being his foil as he worked out his oral autobiography. And, if the truth be told, I was interested, more than willing to submit to Milton's way with a tale, for hours on end, till sundown and sun-up. One of these times, Milton told me a story of his youth which, as he explained, was a key to his relationship with women, the leitmotif, as it were, of his relationships for the rest of his life.

"I was once in love with an older woman," he began, as we sat on a bench in the sun on the southern slope of Mont Royal. "In fact, she was our neighbour, an enormous whale of a woman who liked to stuff the local kids full of her home-made cookies, and who also liked to undress for bed without drawing the curtains. Being eleven or twelve years of age, I was much interested in watching this nightly ritual from my bedroom window, face perched on the ledge as I knelt on my bed, lights out. Better than the drive-in theatre, I thought, as Mrs. Gervais revealed her far from winsome girth, unaware of my hidden gaze.

"One summer day during this period of my life, my mother asked me to light the barbecue, a little circular affair with three legs, in the backyard. As I passed out the screen door onto the patio, I noticed Mrs. Gervais had set out her laundry on the line. A rather stiff wind was filling her sheets and under-clothes, strong enough to snap them, in fact. Like most boys of that age I was completely lacking in intelligence, and whatever innate intelligence I had inherited as a young child had long since been burned off by a steady diet of Twinkies and Nestlé's Quik chocolate powder eaten dry by the spoonful. At any rate, the danger of mixing fire and high wind never surged to the forefront of my brain. I soaked the charcoal briquets in lighter fluid as I had been taught by my father. I even took a certain pride in being capable of handling such materials, of being privy to the raw knowledge reserved for the male of the species. In our neighbourhood, mothers never ever lit the barbecue, or cut the grass.

"I lit my carefully constructed pyramid and watched the flames slither up and release an oily cloud on the breeze... directly into the clean white wash of Mrs. Gervais. Although I felt badly about that, it bothered me for only a moment, the smoke soon dissipating as the coals began to grow white-hot, more quickly than usual, in fact, urged on by the stiff wind.

"Settling back into a lawn chair, I watched with a certain sinister delight as a pair of underpants on the line shimmied in the wind. All sorts of illicit images flapped out of those enormous, billowy bags. I relished the chance to fill them up again with whatever I could imagine. I wallowed in this juvenile sewer for a few luscious minutes, the underpants, a mere fifteen feet away, stiff as a sail in the breeze. Deciding it was time to spread the coals into an even bed, I took a metal poker used for this purpose, jabbed the glowing pyramid and watched it collapse... just as the strongest wind yet lifted some of the bits of white-hot charcoal

69

and blew them into the nearby laundry. The crotch of Mrs. Gervais' underpants must have been the repository of a particularly large chunk, for they immediately burst into flames. I looked at them as if I were in a dream, or as if my dreams had taken life, exposing my deepest thoughts to the world, a world which would surely not understand. I watched stunned as her flaming underpants ignited the other six pairs of underpants along the line. Then the sheets. Finally the word leapt from my mouth. 'Fire!' I screamed, turning for the house. 'T-bone steaks,' my mother sang as she came through the screen door with a platter of meat, thinking I had just informed her that the barbecue was ready. Then she saw the line on fire, dropped the platter and ran for my father. It ended with my father holding a garden hose on the charred ruins of Mrs. Gervais' most intimate apparel. They all looked at me and I sensed without the flicker of a doubt that they all knew, my parents, Mr. and Mrs. Gervais, a few neighbourhood kids, they all knew in their way that my own self-indulgent imagination had ignited her underpants. That night, she drew the curtains.''

Half-asleep in my bed in London, I sat up with a start on remembering one other small point Milton had mentioned when he told me this story: he said Mrs. Gervais always smelled faintly of an odd fragrance, like juniper smoke.

CHAPTER V

1.

In the back room of the deli on Sherbrooke Street, Milton stared at his pastrami sandwich. He lifted up the top half of the kaiser roll and looked inside. "You see, the Iliad isn't about war and a beautiful woman at all. It's about the nature of fire, and time's wick burning down. The fire of anger, the fire of jealousy, the fire of desire. The fire of purification and initiation, the fire of transcendence, the fires of the imagination. That story I told you about my neighbour's wash on the line — it had to do with my initiation, Alex. Puberty is the time when you learn about fire in its myriad forms. You are reborn into your own sex, your own gender. Your new relationship with woman begins with a separation from woman. And don't forget that most primitives believe fire comes from the genitals of woman. Man had to steal it from her. Shamans are supposed to have power over fire, but fire is just a symbol, really, for all those other charged aspects of reality. The Tibetan adept, too, has power over fire, and can protect himself from the elements with inner heat, live naked in the snow." He paused, closed the kaiser and sat back.

"You know, Alex," I could tell Milton was about to launch into one of his patented non sequiturs — "I'm about to contradict myself, but life is filled with contradictions. I just do not understand this addiction you have to mysterious, far-away places. I have the same addiction, of course, but I would like to hear how you justify yours. I mean, for god's sake, Alex, who cares about Tibet, who cares about Ottley's high leather riding boots which he caresses obsessively, who cares about Candler's adventures...?"

Already well into a steak sandwich which turned out to be much tougher than I had expected, I had some difficulty replying. However, my strenuous masticating gave me time to think of an answer. "Okay," I garbled, swallowing heavily, "okay, okay, I've got it. I don't care about all that stuff either, not really. It's all just endless conceptual garbage, empty. And yet...and yet..." I took another bite.

Milton's left elbow was on the table, chin resting in palm, right fingers with their long fingernails like those of a medieval alchemist picking sesame seeds off the kaiser and eating them one by one. "And yet...?" He looked up at me.

My mouth was full again. Chewing and thinking, the same process. "Because it's empty, you can see it more clearly," I finally blurted out.

"What?" he said, tossing me a quizzical look, forehead wrinkling, the kind of look I used to get when I tried to explain Nietzsche to my mother.

"Okay, okay," I calmed myself, "I see I'm going to have to explain everything. You see, Milton, I don't care about Tibet or Candler or even language itself, and because I don't care, well then, I can really care." I stopped. The more I tried to explain my position, the deeper I sank in the mire. He smiled and prepared to watch the top of my head sink slowly into the quicksand, enjoying my struggle. I decided I had to stumble on, like an enemy of the Mafia in Palermo who is tied in such a way that his own struggle to break free forces him to choke himself. I sighed. "A long time ago, when I was a young man," I said, "I had collected an enormous pile of writing, oh, it was wonderful writing, every word of it a delight to the eye and ear. There was just one problem with this pile of beautiful words I had squeezed from my pen: it was choking me, like too many children underfoot, like a great fat woman stuffed with millions of little fetuses, an awesome succubus sitting on my chest sucking my life out. I took those notebooks and burned them, making a marvellous conflagration outside my cabin in the country. I felt wonderful, utterly liberated. I could breathe. And then the very next day, before the ashes had even cooled, I wrote a word down; actually, it must have started with a letter, a single letter. And that word stretched into a line and then a page, I couldn't help myself, I was a man obsessed, and that page became ten pages, twenty, thirty...and the next day I wrote again and after three months I had another pile to burn and burn it I did, for it had turned into a demon again, weighing on me, choking me. After that I didn't write for six months, but I started again eventually when I thought I had been cured. But I wasn't cured — it's somewhat better now, but that succubus with her yammering that pierces my ears and her tongue dripping honey and vinegar still weighs on me, still sits on my face." I was getting carried away, the man and wife at the next table were staring at me, Milton, who was still listening, looked again under the top of his kaiser, and finally I breathed deeply and sighed.

"Some story," Milton said. "You're really crazy."

"Anyway," I added, "I'm tired of trying to figure it out. If it weren't writing, something else would become my obsession — the track, lotteries, making money, whatever."

"True enough."

Looking towards the deli's front window piled high with glass jars of pickles, I noticed that snow had started to fall outside, large soft flakes drifting down as if in a dream.

It seemed that Milton was reading my mind when he said, smiling, "I wonder how Candler is doing in those high mountains?"

2.

Staring at the ground as he approached Young-husband's tent, Candler pondered the weird journey of which he was a part and yet not a part. It seemed as if the entire journey were a process of exfoliation, a process of stripping bare. And not only for himself. Each day as they drew closer to Lhasa, every man in the expedition seemed to grow more raw. Candler felt as if his skin were being peeled back, as if the ritual in front of the fire with Sarge had put into process an evolution from which he could not escape. He passed Macdonald's tent and heard a deep, cavernous hacking. The general was a strong man; there were rumours circulating that mentioned his exploits in China, the chances he had taken, the fellow officers he had ruined. And yet the man was sinking deeper every day and insisted on trying to keep control of what was called the Mission Escort, for this was not, strictly speaking, an invasion but an attempt to force diplomatic contact with the Dalai Lama. For Ottley, though, Candler thought, as he saw the horses shifting in a temporary enclosure in the early morning light, this is definitely an invasion. The fact was Ottley was really in control of the military end of the operation. He had General Macdonald's ear. He could do no wrong.

Ottley too had begun to show the strain of the campaign, losing his temper over trifles, threatening to have a Gurkha hanged the previous evening for not shining his boots properly. Perhaps it was the altitude or the strangeness of it all, but this trudge to Lhasa past a seemingly endless line of dead pack animals and Tibetan bone-gardens was stripping Ottley raw too, although his reaction to that development was more aggression, more anger, more stupidity. The previous week he had had a Tibetan flogged with a cat-o'-nine-tails. The man was suspected of being a spy. Suspected! When his relatives came to claim him he was half-dead, lying face down in dust and blood.

Even Colonel Younghusband, Candler thought as he neared the tent, the great mystery of the group, begins to show it. His correct, military bearing reveals no sign of wavering, yet his blue eyes show the strain. He's torn — between fulfilling his diplomatic function and having to resort to military carnage. His eyes are sad and wet and hard to look at, as if his very soul were being exposed. Younghusband has remained a loner through the entire expedition, keeping his distance from all, partly because of his superior rank, but more due to his character. I cannot seem to touch the man, can't get close to him. He never quite comes down to a human level with the rest of us, and yet he too is being stripped bare, like this raw land with its grey jutting cliffs and its rubble of stone fragments strewn as far as the eye can see. And today he has asked me to ride with him. I wonder what is up, Candler thought, as he pulled back the flap of the tent.

3.

In the brisk mountain air, clouds of breath could be seen emanating from the nostrils of the horses. Ephemeral clouds that existed for a moment only and then disappeared into nothingness.

The force was in a wide valley, making its way for the only tree in the distance, which stood hard by a flat river sparkling in the stony-brilliant daylight. To Candler's immediate left, Younghusband rode in silence. Behind, Sarge followed on a small Tibetan pony and behind him the rest of the column stretched across the plain in stuttering sections of cavalry, foot-soldiers and artillery. A full two-thirds of the column was made up of pack animals and coolies under mounted guard on the flanks. The great unspoken fear for every man along the line was the fear of being cut off, the fear of being left on his own to fend for himself in this inhospitable land of stone and snow.

Beyond the end of the column they knew the line continued, all the way to England in a sense, for a corps of engineers was busy installing a telegraph wire the way they had come, doing their best to keep the expedition linked to India and the outside world. Among the Tibetans, Candler learned, it was believed the telegraph line was there so the invaders could find their way back. The common soldiers bellowed when they heard this, but Candler thought, in one sense, it was true.

They were riding into the unknown, although they ordered the chaos of land and sky ahead of them with words they knew: mountain, cloud, river, town. Yet the ineffable emptiness surrounding those words made them appear to be swallowed up by the sheer immensity and strangeness of the land. Candler felt they couldn't come to know it — not as it really was, not as they were. They, or rather he, had to change, utterly. They weren't invading Tibet — they were being swallowed.

Younghusband kept his clear blue eyes fixed on the tree in the distance. "You may wonder, Candler, why I have asked you to ride with me today." The colonel spoke with the prestigious accent called Received Pronunciation, although he used it in a slightly less clipped manner than many of his class. "I am seeking your opinion as an independent observer. What do you think of our expedition?" He added quickly, glancing at the journalist, "I expect you to be thoroughly honest with me — you have nothing to fear."

"Do you play chess, sir?"

"Yes, Candler, I do."

"This expedition, Colonel, seems to me like a game of chess played against an invisible opponent. It seems as if we are playing in one room while the Tibetans play on a completely separate board in another room. Neither side sees the other's moves."

"Are you saying we do not understand each other?"

"It's more than that. I can't put my finger on it. Perhaps we don't have the least inkling of how they think. Even their wounded and dying do not react as one would expect. Sometimes they seem to have the stunned calm of, well, animals, sir."

"Animals?"

"Yes. I have been observing Lieutenant Bailey's animals, and they seem to have a certain resignation that the Tibetans share."

The colonel thought. The sound of the horses' hooves kept a steady rhythm on the hard-packed, crusted snow. "In this game of chess, Mr. Candler, who is black and who is white?"

Candler cleared his throat. "I don't know the answer to that any more. I thought I knew once but...I don't know any more."

They rode on in silence. "We will be arriving at Gyantse late this afternoon," the colonel observed. "We are likely to be there a while — it appears to be the largest town on our route and my scouts inform me it's well-fortified. Have you seen General Macdonald these past few days, Mr. Candler?"

"Yes, I have."

"And what do you think, Mr. Candler?"

"To be honest, Colonel, I believe the ghost is upon him but he won't admit it."

"This land weighs heavily upon him. He is a strong man, though a fool. Do you know what is said about fools, Mr. Candler?"

"No, what is that, Colonel?"

"Fools in the mountains are soon swallowed up."

Candler turned half in his saddle and looked back along the long line of troops. "Perhaps we are all being swallowed."

4.

So much happens by accident. This could be called magic but we prefer to call it accident. I had not seen Auntie Liz for a long time. Sitting at her dark mahogany dining-room table with its legs ending in what appeared to be carvings of lion paws, I leaned over a cup of tea.

"No milk?" she remarked.

"Just sugar," I said.

"Oh my, you are a barbarian," she smirked, sipping, little finger extended, grey bun at the back of her head.

The words "sealing wax" had prompted this visit to Auntie Liz. I had chanced upon the words in my readings in the British Library and I looked up into the cavernous vault to watch the words reverberate in the bell of that room, ringing round and round and round. And then it struck me: Candler's journey, Younghusband's expedition, was marching there like a frieze running round the base of the dome. They weren't getting anywhere, they weren't moving — the mountains, like time, were marching through them, moving through their minds like clouds. The light pouring through the grand windows at the dome's base illumined a history that repeated itself over and over again, like a thought, like the memory of a woman's face, a memory that won't leave you.

"Do you have any sealing wax?" I asked Auntie Liz.

"Yes, of course." She rose to fetch it from its place in a drawer. It was as if someone asked her for sealing wax every day. She removed a carved box, rosewood, I believe, with little intaglioed pineapples on it. It slid open. Inside, laid out in pleasing stacks, were bars of wax. At one end, in a separate compartment, was a marble seal.

Taking it out, I turned it over. It was a scorpion.

My aunt leaned forward and took it from my hand. "It was a gift from my mother, in the family for years," she whispered, putting it hastily away.

5.

"My dear wife," Edmund Candler wrote, "we have come to rest, after much difficult travelling, in a town called Gyantse, fair-sized, with a well-secured fort on a hill nearby. I believe we will have our best fight yet.

"You will recall I mentioned my manservant, Sarge, and what an unusual fellow he is. I trust him greatly. Tonight, after dinner, he showed me something quite odd. It was a letter he had, in a silk envelope, the wax seal broken. As he pulled the fine parchment from the envelope, he treated it as if it were something of

81

great value. And well he should have. It was a letter from Lord Curzon himself, addressed to the Dalai Lama! I was astounded. Our entire presence here may have something to do with the fact that this letter was never delivered. It was dated June 6, 1901. Lord Curzon had written: 'I wish to impress on Your Holiness that, whilst I retain the desire to enter into friendly relations with yourself, and to promote a better understanding between the two nations, yet if no attempt is made to reciprocate these feelings, and if, on the contrary, they are treated with rudeness and indifference, my government must reserve their right to take such steps as may seem to them necessary and proper to enforce the terms of the Treaty, and to ensure that the Trade Regulations are observed.' I could not believe my eyes as I read it! Actually the wording may have been slightly different — I write it now from memory.

"At my urging, Sarge, smiling all the while, seeming to scoff at my excitement, told me where he had obtained the letter. Apparently it had been handed to a Bhutanese official for delivery to Lhasa. This official, Ugyen Kazi, was delivering some animals to the Dalai Lama for his private zoo. Two elephants, two peacocks and a leopard, in fact. When one of the elephants died en route, Kazi decided to allow his subordinates to deliver the other beasts, not wishing to incur the wrath of the Dalai Lama's steely minister, Dorjieff, for losing one of the beasts. He forgot about the letter. Sometime later, he met Sarge on the road. They became friends for a short while as they travelled together and when their roads diverged, Ugyen Kazi handed the letter to Sarge for delivery, for he knew the latter was headed for Lhasa. Sarge explained that his own plans changed several days later, due to a massive avalanche blocking the pass. He headed south instead with several itinerant monks and spent the summer months at a monastery. Such is the movement of time in Tibet that he is only just now on his way back with the letter to Lhasa. It is very strange — we English are put in the position of delivering the blow before the threat.

"When I said that we must show this letter to Young-husband, who would surely be angry to hear the tale and to see that the sealed letter, a private letter after all, had been violated, Sarge snatched it from my hand and threw it in the pine fire, along with the envelope. He laughed and said we English would never under-stand anything. Then Ottley was at the door asking what was going on, in his snappish way.

"Something made me answer differently than I had planned, perhaps because it was Ottley, whom I despise, as you know. If it had been Younghusband, I believe I would have behaved otherwise. I told him that it was nothing and to be on his way. I spoke gruffly and motioned him off, saying nothing about the letter. Though he left scowling, I believe I did right. I believe we will go to Lhasa one way or the other. The Tibetans are doomed to their fate and we are doomed to ours. (I will add to this letter tomorrow or the next day. Until then, my love...)"

6.

Dorjieff's eyes, mere slits in his large round head, never stopped moving. A wide nose and bulbous cheeks made him appear younger than his fifty years. His plain long robe accentuated his stockiness while its wide sleeves hid his hands. A small cloth cap topped his hairless head.

At the end of a long hallway, he whispered to a shadowy figure, another monk, but one dressed quite differently. A door to their left opened and they slipped through into a resplendent hall lit by chandeliers.

"Tsar Nicholas II and the Tsarina," Rasputin introduced them and Dorjieff bowed.

"I bring greetings and a rare gift from His Holiness the Dalai Lama," Dorjieff announced, pulling a wrapped piece of folded fabric from beneath his robes and offering it to the seated Tsar.

The Tsar tore at the paper and soon revealed an intricate Chinese embroidery depicting a river scene with two boats, a wading crane and a pair of ducks in flight. In one corner was an inscription in Chinese. This caught the Tsar's attention more than the embroidery itself.

"Ah, His Holiness has given me a new title," he enthused. "Already he has named me Stepson of Heaven and 169th Reincarnation. What is this one, good Dorjieff? Tell me, tell me," he insisted, pointing to the inscription.

Dorjieff was aghast. What should he do? Tell the Tsar that the inscription was, in fact, the Chinese advertisement of a Shanghai firm? He hesitated.

"Is it so unspeakable, Dorjieff?" the Tsar pressed him. "So mystical it cannot be spoken in the presence of these others." He gestured at the attendants. "We will have them removed." The merest look from the corner of his eye sent Rasputin into action. Soon the hall was empty but for the two monks, the emperor and his lady.

"If I am to be the protector of all Buddhist Asia, Dorjieff, I must have my name. Now speak. What has the Dalai Lama honoured me with, Tse-nyi-ken-po?" the Tsar asked, using Dorjieff's own title, the Abbot of Metaphysics.

The title "Stepson of Hell" flashed through Dorjieff's mind even as he said, bowing, "Seventh Mystic of Darkness, Your Majesty."

The Tsar sighed, looking fondly at the inscription. Rasputin cast Dorjieff a dark questioning look.

7.

"What amazes me, Milton," I said, "is how things are so much more connected than we realize. I mean, here we are, looking at Tibet at the turn of the century through the small end of the telescope and it seems so distant and untouchable. But then you realize while Dorjieff was plotting with Rasputin to control the Buddhist world for Nicholas, on the other side of

St. Petersburg, Igor Stravinsky was studying music with Rimsky-Korsakov. Dorjieff and Stravinsky could have passed each other on the street. Years later Stravinsky ends up living outside Los Angeles, for god's sake, where he dies in 1971. I mean I could have sat in a seat at O'Hare Airport in Chicago in 1967 next to Stravinsky who passed Dorjieff in St. Petersburg. Suddenly the world seems amazingly small."

Milton took a pull on his scotch, caramel-coloured, smoky Glenlivet. He gazed at his left thumbnail. "Small, yes, quite small," he agreed.

8.

Bailey's home-made kite, blood-red against the blue sky, alternately tugged and pranced like a small pet dog over the tumbledown houses of Gyantse. A gaggle of Tibetan urchins watched in amazement. Candler stood with his one good hand shading his eyes, the other sleeve pinned and empty. Sarge gazed up, squinting.

Several hundred yards away, across the stubbled field in which they stood, a bazaar of Tibetan merchants clamoured, sprinkled here and there with tall Gurkhas browsing, British soldiers, bearded, turbaned Sikhs, a few excited shaven-headed monks and the odd Bhutanese or Nepali trader far from home.

The town of Gyantse seemed to stumble down the stony hill, which was topped by a fortified bastion, or *jong*. The squarish houses of the town ended at the edge of the marketplace field. At the other extremity of the field stood a cluster of dwellings in a grove of graceful willow trees next to a river sparkling with light. At this point on the river, an arcing stone bridge curved over into a fertile field.

Gyantse was, in a sense, the culmination of a ten-mile-long valley, unusually rich and thoroughly cultivated. The valley held a total of thirty-three villages, Gyantse the largest, at the northeastern end, where the road to Lhasa left the valley and re-entered the hills. High on the cliffs of surrounding mountains perched the structures of the Seven Monasteries, as if brooding over the scene.

Compared to most of the harsh land they had passed through, Gyantse was lovely, soft, a fertile oasis in the midst of broken country and unremitting mountains whose beauty was of a kind hard and untouchable. The valley, however, was beauty on a human scale, brought down to earth, something one could pass through, caress, smell. And that is why, Candler thought, one could mistakenly take it for granted.

The friendliness of the local people was a surprise and a welcome relief. They came out to sell butter, eggs, vegetables and meat to the expedition, as well as bright woven carpets and stone images of the Buddhas and others of their gods. The men enjoyed gazing at the young women who sold goods. Candler too found many of them beautiful, despite their charcoal-blackened faces. It was in their eyes, soft and swimming as warm ponds, and in the gentle sway of their bodies. They seemed to him at one with the peaceful, lush valley.

Lieutenant Bailey exhibited all the exuberance of youth as he ran across the field, almost being lifted into the air by the vigorous kite. The children followed in a swarm, laughing, pointing and jabbering.

At first the expeditionary force had taken over the fortified *jong*, but the structure was half-ruin and extremely filthy, so Younghusband and Macdonald had decided that they should take up residence in the cluster of dwellings in the grove which was gladly rented to the expedition by a local landowner.

Rumours abounded that the Dalai Lama had decided on a treaty to settle the affair and would soon send his emissaries to Gyantse to discuss terms with Younghusband. The peaceful attitude of the townspeople lent credence to the rumours. Thus it was decided that General Macdonald would return to Chumbi with the greater part of the force, there being too little room in the cluster of buildings dubbed "the mission." As well, the departure would ease the difficulties of supply this far up the line. It appeared that peace had broken out along with clusters of early spring flowers.

Candler and Sarge wandered into the bazaar, a ramshackle collection of goods spread out on blankets on the ground, rough stalls, wandering yaks, scurrying dogs, boisterous traders and untethered children.

"Perhaps I shall buy one of their Buddhas," Candler mentioned to Sarge, who nodded.

They wandered on, the correspondent watching for the right statue, eyeing rows of them set out for display.

Sarge touched his arm. "Look...I believe she has something for you."

Candler glanced up to see a young woman walking towards them, a rough cloth bag in her arms. She walked directly up to Candler, smiling. He halted and watched as she opened the bag, took out an object and handed it to him. Turning to Sarge, she said a few words in Tibetan. "For you," he said to Candler, who felt its stone weight in his hand. "A carving...a gift." Candler glanced at it. In that moment, the young woman disappeared into the crowd. The object was wrapped in a plain brown cloth and tied tightly with string. It was obvious to Candler, even through the cloth, that it was a small stone Buddha, about the size of his fist. He felt its weight again, dragging him down to earth, felt it pushing the soles of his feet against the ground. The way the string was wrapped around and around the shoulders, waist, legs and neck of the carving made it seem like it was a bound prisoner, or perhaps something of great power kept under containment. He started to open it. Sarge touched his hand. "No...do not open here. Wait until you are in your own land. Believe me." His look was hard and uncompromising. Candler stopped opening the package. Once again he felt its weight, sensed the bound power there and wondered.

Suddenly, there was a strange hubbub around him. "Look," Sarge shouted. Candler glanced up and noticed everyone else in the bazaar was also gazing upward. Bailey's kite string had snapped. The blood-red kite was sailing higher and higher over the town. High above the kite, drifting in watchful circles, was a huge eagle, moving along with the kite, always keeping above, as if protecting it.

CHAPTER VI

—————— • ◦ • ——————

1.

They rested in Gyantse, awaiting the Dalai Lama's emissaries, awaiting the return of General Macdonald with fresh supplies. What they did not know was that Macdonald always felt in great spirits when he was headed down the line. But a simple shift of the head, the mere thought of turning towards Lhasa, brought the weight of the Himalayas on his back. Macdonald delayed in Chumbi. Perhaps he would not be needed. Perhaps the entire affair would be settled.

In Gyantse, Younghusband and his men had mixed feelings. The earnest wish to settle the ridiculous little affair mixed uneasily with a longing to carry it out to its conclusion, to reach Lhasa, to experience all the wonders about which they had heard rumours.

In the middle of the town of Gyantse stood a golden-roofed temple. The gold shone in the afternoon sun with such a clarity it would almost lift the viewer off his feet. To the men, it became a symbol of the opulent riches and wonders they imagined awaited them in Lhasa. No one actually spoke of it but somehow the idea had taken root. If anyone mentioned Lhasa in conversation, he would be sure to glance surreptitiously towards the gold roof in their midst.

Sarge noticed this. He mentioned it to Candler. "These fools — willing to trade blood for gold . . . their own blood and the blood of others. But they will continue to Lhasa — in their blindness. And they will see nothing there, just as they see nothing here. Perhaps it is meant to be — we will infect them with a disease they will never be free of."

"What do you mean?" Candler asked.

"I like you English," Sarge grinned, evasively.

The next day, in the middle of the afternoon, Younghusband and Ottley rode down from the hills back into camp. On the back of Ottley's mount was spread the body of a small deer, a hole in its throat, its blood running in a trickle down the flank and leg of Ottley's horse.

As they approached the mission, Captain Hodgson met them on foot. He saluted.

"Queer happenings, sir."

"What's that?" Ottley said.

They soon learned that Sarge had taken up a position sitting cross-legged on top of a huge boulder between the mission and the town.

"He's been sitting there all day. Not moving," Hodgson explained. "It's giving the men the creeps, sir."

Nothing anyone said nor even the lobbing of a few pebbles could make the Tibetan come down. In fact, he had not moved at all for six hours.

A gusty wind had started to stir the dust around the camp. The donkeys in their enclosure seemed uneasy. Ottley's horse snuffled and stamped.

"I'll get him down" — Ottley drew out his rifle.

Younghusband looked over. "Leave him alone," he ordered crisply and rode on to his quarters.

Later that evening, Sarge and Candler talked quietly.

"I fear for this valley," Sarge said. "It has always known nothing but peace. The people here do not know what it means to water their fields with blood, to lose their sons."

Sarge was busily serving tea to the correspondent who held a pen in his hand, trying to give the readers of the *Daily Mail* some idea of what Gyantse was like. It seemed an impossible task. They would be sitting at a table staring out at grey London, picking up and putting down their cups of tea, one moment reading of far-off Gyantse, Tibet, the next moment checking the race results.

"I travelled much in China in my youth," Sarge continued. "There were places where war had been going on so long that the earth was as much bones as soil. Farmers had to plant their seeds in the eye-sockets of skulls and between rows of ribs."

Candler looked up. "Perhaps tomorrow the emissaries will bring peace from Lhasa."

"Peace from Lhasa? How would that be possible? No one will bring peace from Lhasa. Is peace an object you can put on the back of a horse and carry from one place to another?" Candler had never before seen Sarge angry. "Idiots. These people are idiots. Your people, my people, all the same." He waved his hand in a gesture of dismissal and stomped out into the gathering dark.

2.

At a certain point in my investigations at seat B4 in the British Library, I realized that the closer I came to Lhasa, the closer Edmund Candler came to Lhasa, the less could I rely on the facts. The official version was no truth. I had to go further and further into the realms of imagination and magic to find the truth, for the truth lay beyond the facts, at the same time including them.

Actually, there were and are three versions to the story. The official version, which Candler sent down the shining telegraph wires back to India and thence to England and the world, was the outer version. It was not a lie and yet merely a portion of the truth. It took advantage of the limits of its medium: what was not stated was not heard by the world. It offered none of the ambiguity of the situation, none of Younghusband's doubt, none of the acute strangeness of the venture, none of the chaos that began to invade the accepted realities of all the men involved in this march to the top of the world.

The doubts and ambiguities were the inner version of the tale. All present shared them but few spoke of them. Each and every man knew he was taking part in something bigger than himself and yet could not give this vague feeling a voice or a form. So this inner version expressed itself as doubt in some, ambiguous feelings in others, sickness or disgust in still others, or even as the thrill of adventure in a few.

There was and is, however, a third version: the secret version. The secret version happens outside time. Younghusband's expedition and Candler's quest are still happening. As Candler would enter the Potala Palace in Lhasa in search of ... what? A good story? Gold? Mystery? So, I, Alex, entered the British Library reading room in search of ... what? A certain book? The one line that turns Candler's quest like a key? A sudden insight?

That a tale could take life was all. That the words chosen were the words chosen because they were the life lived. It meant the towers built by Tibet's great poet, Milarepa, which were destroyed a thousand times for no reason at the behest of his teacher, Marpa, and this book had a purpose after all, but that purpose was immediate and unnamable. Even after walking the crest of the mountains into Lhasa, Candler would find nothing there.

3.

Each of them had his own version of Lhasa, what it promised, what was waiting there, in the distance, on the roof of the world. Candler's was different than Younghusband's which was quite different than Lieutenant Bailey's which was diametrically opposed to Macdonald's. Each version was its own, a complex of hopes, fears, duties, dreams and imaginings.

For Candler, Lhasa was the promise of an unveiling. Despite everything, he still expected to find something there, something astounding and ineffable, the shining heart of mystery, though Sarge had warned him repeatedly to expect nothing. Sarge had said it was a town like any other, full of suffering and easy pleasure.

For Candler's wife, Veronica, far off in England, Lhasa was another woman, seducing Edmund further and further from her. That is how she thought of this city that was the goal of Candler's journey. Little did she know that, despite the distance, she was as close to Lhasa as anyone else.

For Younghusband, Lhasa was a city of officialdom, the place where this insane country would come together, would begin to make sense. It was the solution to the riddle, the final piece of a contorted, vertical puzzle. Although he had strong reservations and enough doubt to turn back a lesser man, he kept his feelings in check out of a clear sense of duty. Of course, he was wrong about everything falling into place.

Lieutenant Bailey had an innocent view of Lhasa. The image in his mind was almost Eden-like; it was a land not unlike the Shambhala of ancient Tibetan culture where animals were sacred and suffering was abolished. He still, however, failed to realize that this kingdom was a projection of his own mind. If he had asked, Sarge could have warned him that Lhasa was far from Shambhala.

The former commander of balloons, Macdonald, took a long pull on his cigarette and thought about Lhasa. A stifling dread settled on his shoulders. Why was all this effort necessary? He feared the city, from his depths. Why? He himself didn't understand. Gold was not in his plans, although, for his men, the imagining of a thousand gold towers was all that kept them tied to the wheel and he did nothing to discourage the rumours.

Sarge, whose name given him by the British was an unwitting acronym of his real Tibetan name, Gesar, had his own version of Lhasa. It was a construction of memories incredibly light and delicate. It was a net of fine jade, strands thin as human hairs, that collapsed at the touch. He spent little time reimagining Lhasa. What was the point? Yet he found the versions of the others intriguing and each correct in its way.

For Ottley, Lhasa was the place where he could have his boots resoled.

Lhasa, for Auntie Liz, was a bit like her memories of a childhood journey to York — far away, filled with strange people and sombre cathedrals, a place for adventurous and foolish young men, a place of vast and profound darkness and brilliant, seductive fire.

For Milton, Lhasa was a book, thick and authoritative, authorship unknown, therefore ancient and beyond questioning.

Lhasa, for me, was the place where words and silence came together.

4.

Candler slept against the wall furthest from the door while Sarge snored just inside the entrance to the room as if he were there to keep guard over the stone threshold. In the distance of the rambling building, there was a sound, a slow, measured knocking. Boots on the stone floor, coming closer, but hardly noticeable at all. The sound stopped, then started again.

A long shadow leaned over Sarge, who was still snoring. The figure bent lower and lower, something in its right hand poised over Sarge's throat.

There was a sudden glint of steel and Candler shot bolt upright from his cot. "Who's there?" he blurted, his voice in the dead of night ringing through the damp stone building. The figure, spinning round, ran through the doorway and disappeared. Candler, more interested in Sarge's welfare, decided not to pursue.

Sarge was sitting up rubbing his eyes. He gave Candler a wide smile. "I think someone tried to kill you," the correspondent said.

"Ottley," returned Sarge, matter-of-factly. "I can smell his boot polish."

"But...why?"

"Because he fears I will kill him if he doesn't kill me first...and he's right." Sarge grinned again.

5.

Seated at his makeshift desk, Candler studied notes in preparation for his next report to the *Daily Mail*.

He could hear Lieutenant Bailey's voice nearby, speaking to...who was it...the expedition artist, Lieutenant Rybot?

"Did you hear what happened at Raratong?" Bailey asked his companion.

"Yes, of course, the fire, a whole shed of supplies lost in several hours. They said it was lightning."

"It *was* lightning, but part of the story has been kept secret. I went down the line with General Macdonald to check out some yaks he wanted to buy. When we got to Raratong, where the provisions were stored — well over a hundred tons — I noticed that the gate to the small horse enclosure had been left open and about a dozen horses were grazing in a nearby meadow. Someone had left it open on purpose, I'm sure of it."

The artist harrumphed.

"And what's more, there *was* a bolt of lightning that hit the shed — but it came out of a perfectly blue sky!"

Candler lifted his pen at overhearing this bit of news. Then a strange thought struck him: Sarge had been gone for two days and a night, only returning in the middle of the night the day after the conflagration.

"What did Macdonald say about it?" the artist asked.

"Macdonald? Macdonald, I believe, was pleased, though he didn't express it too widely. Anything that keeps him moving away from Lhasa pleases him. I think he would much prefer to be back with his balloon corps in China."

Later, the correspondent confronted Sarge. He knew he was taking a gargantuan leap into the preposterous but he went ahead: "Why did you cause lightning to strike the supplies at Raratong if it is our fate to go to Lhasa anyway?"

A glance of anger sparked in Sarge's eyes, then it quickly softened into a sparkle. "Ah, you are learning, Englishman. Good, good, that is very good. You begin to see a little more clearly. It is also my fate to make the journey a difficult one so that it will have some value, so that it will be memorable — for you and all the others too. However, the possibility that I may contradict myself worries me not in the least."

6.

April 18, 1904   Gyantse   13,070 feet

I carry the mountains with me all the time, hovering high up behind all that I do, all that I think, dream, imagine, say, believe, hope for and fear, always there unchanging, towering and white, a presence that is absolutely still, a kind of three-dimensional screen for the light to play on, the sunset coating silver peaks and slopes with red lacquer or dawn bringing out a hue like young, healthy flesh, but this is all a play of light, like emotions projected on a vast emptiness of brilliant stone, it never moves, it never changes, it says nothing, is utterly clear and solid and untouchable. The mountain. Someday I will realize the mountain is my heart.

7.

When Colonel Ottley once again shot a deer in the nearby hills, rather than sling the animal over the back of his horse, he tied a rope to the deer's hind legs and dragged it along the dusty trail leading to the town and the military compound. Sarge squatted in the stubble outside the low stone building that served as the men's sleeping quarters and watched as, in the distance, a cloud of dust rose from behind the horse and rider and dissipated in the mid-afternoon light. The rider kept coming. He passed near the compound and approached the field where the open-air market was crowded as usual with townspeople, merchants and a few farmers and yak-herders down from the surrounding hills.

As Ottley passed the compound, Candler happened to come up next to Sarge and noticed that the rider was the colonel and that he was dragging the corpse of a deer towards the market field. They watched to see what he would do.

The people in the marketplace stopped their activities and stood in silence. Sombre, dark clouds were descending, hiding the crests of the nearest mountains beyond the town. Rather than stop at the edge of the market, the colonel rode straight up the main market street, knocking over a stall of vegetables and nearly trampling a child who was slow in moving out of the way. The deer behind was streaming blood from several rough wounds, blood that mixed with the dust of the market street. Ottley passed boldly, menacingly, through the market and, on coming to the far end, pulled up his horse, turned and rode through again, as if showing off his prize. After he had passed through, he turned hard left and circled the entire market field on its outer perimeter, letting the deer be beaten into a bloody pulp on the stones.

Even from a distance, Candler and Sarge could see several young men in the market go rigid with anger. Also, by this time, half a dozen ragged, dust-coloured dogs were chasing the horse and rider, taking rips at the deer. Ottley pulled up at the entrance to the market. Jumping down from his horse, he pulled out a long knife and slit the rope with one upward sweep. Then he watched as the dogs jumped into the deer, devouring it.

8.

For many weeks, I had avoided seeing Auntie Liz. Perhaps I sensed that those steel blue eyes that could hold one in their grip were fading to rheumy grey. At any rate, I went at her special request, she having telephoned me early on a Wednesday evening. How strange to hear her voice with its own built-in static crackling over the line. I promised to drop round after dinner the next evening.

My knock was answered by a distant cousin of mine whom I vaguely recognized. I also recalled that he was a medical doctor.

"Harold, how are you?" We shook hands.

"Arnold," he corrected me. "Harold is my brother, two years older."

I immediately remembered that I disliked him — one could tell at a glance that he was one of those insufferable officious types — but I was well beyond the point of being embarrassed by my own lapses of memory.

"Oh well, one name is as good as another," I blurted.

He glared at me. "Really, Alex?" he weasled.

"Where's Auntie Liz?" I changed the subject.

"Asleep in her chair, I'm afraid, old boy."

I only had a moment to regret having come and to shiver with distaste at possibly having to spend an inordinate amount of time with Arnold or Harold or whoever he was, when her weak voice called from the parlour: "Alex, is that you?"

I entered. She sat in a large easy chair, a grey blanket of itchy-looking wool on her lap.

"How are you?"

She proceeded to tell me, going into rather too much detail concerning her failing liver, the ineptitude of doctors, the kindness of my cousin, the horrors of tubes and needles and what was going in and out of them, the uncleanliness of hospitals and her undying need for a good belt of scotch, now forbidden her. This last was really the point of her digressions and what she needed to get off her mind.

As she spoke, I noted, like a small-town storekeeper ticking prices, the profusion of objects on the stand next to her overstuffed chair. First, the lamp at the rear of the dark mahogany table, hung with three rings of cut-glass crystals. The velvet shade had a pastoral scene on it which made me think of the line: "Under the damask dark willows and purple osiers." A small glass half-filled with thick, viscous, purplish liquid was next to an unused marble ashtray banded in gold with a gold flange for holding the cigarette. Then, in no apparent order: the Holy Bible, its ribbon bookmark I estimated to be at the beginning of Revelations; a vial of pills; a hand-mirror and brush, both in tortoiseshell; an open tube of pale red lipstick with hardly a tongue-tip left in it; a postcard of the Holy Family.

This last made me recall the crucifix I had seen on one of my previous visits. It hung on a wall in the breadbox-sized kitchen. Auntie Liz had explained that small crowds of three or four in the cramped cubicle had caused the crucifix to tumble numerous times onto the floor. In fact, she had added, any time more than one person was in the room (usually at Christmas or Easter), the crucifix was sure to end up falling, the sudden unconscious nudge of a padded shoulder causing Christ to replay his tumbles on the Stations of the Cross many more than the requisite three times. All these precipitous descents had loosened the tiny nails holding Christ's hands to the wood of the cross. Eventually both nails disappeared under the stove or fridge or some other lost place. Auntie Liz's solution, since she possessed no vials of tiny nails to keep His beloved hands in their righteous place, was to Scotch-tape the poor devil's paws to the cross. Such indignity He must have felt! No more stigmata! Saints of the future would have tape burns instead, strange hairless strips on their wrists. It mattered not in the least to Auntie Liz. The tape worked, therefore it was good. A thoroughly secular logic.

"But I did not call you here to complain." She brought me out of my reverie. "I want to give you something."

Turning, she reached behind the lamp.

"Oh," I said, looking.

In both knobby hands she held out to me Candler's statue of the Buddha. For a moment I hesitated. "For me?" I asked.

"Yes, take it."

I felt as if I were receiving much more than a statue. One is handed a dozen things a day: a newspaper, a pound note, a book — a hundred things a week, a thousand things a month, and yet, once in a while, the action of receiving something is fraught with possible responsibility. I almost refused, knowing there was more here than a simple gift.

"I wonder where the hand is?" I mused, holding the slightly flawed Buddha in my palms.

"Maybe it's in Candler's old trunk in the attic," Auntie Liz chirped brightly.

"You have a chest of his?" I gasped.

Within moments, I stood in the attic staring into an old travelling trunk, completely and utterly empty.

Candler went into his trunk, looking for a can of boot-blacking. At the bottom in the corner, he noticed the package. Taking it out, he felt again its weight. Perhaps it's not a heathen statue after all, he thought, perhaps it's a precious stone. I must see it.

Suddenly, a sound at the door interrupted him. Sarge filled the doorway. He said nothing as he watched Candler place the package, unopened, back in the trunk.

CHAPTER VII

———— ✦ ————

1.

At some point in our relationship I began to realize that Milton was a teller of tales and little more, a person for whom stories were more real than so-called reality, a person for whom the life of the imagination was the only real life and real life merely a lower form of imaginary invention. Once he told me that among the Greeks a natural leader of men was chosen by his ability as a "speaker of tales." Achilles, for example, whom we think of being a leader because of his abilities as a warrior, was actually a leader because he had a superior ear and an aptitude for epic hexameter. Milton too was more than just an entertainer. When he told a tale, it was seamless, as if the room had been swept out and rearranged, as if the clocks had been reset and set ticking to another time. When he was in a particularly jocose mood, his favourite tale, which I heard him expound on three or four festive occasions, usually after more than a soupçon of uplifting drink, dealt with his Uncle George.

Uncle George lived with his wife, Mildred, in an ancient Victorian house on one of the older streets of Ottawa. George worked for the government. Milton was unsure which department — sometimes he swore it was Public Works, which puts a certain ironic twist into the tale. However, it might have been External Affairs.

George's father-in-law, Mildred's father, lived with the family in the three-storey house that was constantly in need of one repair or another. If it wasn't the roof, it was the cellar. If it wasn't the plumbing, it was the wiring. The house, which seemed a good idea at first, had become the bane of George's existence. Gus, Mildred's father, helped where he could, but his knowledge was limited to masonry, which he had studied as a young apprentice. Eventually, he had opted to become a greengrocer instead.

In later years, Gus's once fine physique had slipped badly. He embraced obesity as if it were a religion, praying to his god three times a day at table and often, when he felt particularly pious, he consumed his god steadily, well into the night.

One evening, George was having his boss and his boss's wife over for dinner. In his early forties, George was making some headway in the civil service but an important position was coming up, a position he wanted. George's boss, the austere Mr. Elroy, and his droll, caustic flagship of a wife, Edna, were difficult guests at the best of times.

Before they arrived, George surveyed the house to see that all was in order. He stopped in the cramped dining room. The table was set for four, the best china, the cloth napkins in brass napkin rings. Checking the enormous chandelier, George noted that none of its many little lights were out. Much too big for this room, he thought of the chandelier. Then he noticed a small damp circle on the ceiling. Oh my, he thought, a leak, a leak! That's all I need. He held his hand under it. No drops. Not actually a leak, just a damp spot. What's above? The bathroom. Hmm.

Racing upstairs to the bathroom, he noted that the toilet was indeed seeping into the floor. I must have that looked at — it'll rot the boards eventually.

Later, in the midst of a fine though not affected meal, a pot roast no doubt, the four diners tried to smile. Mr. Elroy's colon was acting up.

"My colon," he explained when Mildred had offered him gravy and he refused. George looked into the gravy boat and imagined Mr. Elroy's colon floating in it. Edna Elroy somehow caught this impertinence.

"Are you expecting an early advancement in your work?" she snidely asked George, knowing full well that the subject, while the centre of attention, was best left unmentioned.

111

"May the best man move up." George swallowed hard, smiling grittily.

"More turnips?" Mildred asked Edna prettily.

"I hate turnips," she said, smiling.

A loud crack came from above.

"How old is this house, George?" Mr. Elroy asked, raising his eyebrows.

"I'd venture about a hundred and fifty years." George looked up.

"Oh my god." Mildred slowly brought her napkin to her mouth as her eyes too went up and her mouth gaped. "The ceiling's giving way."

A ragged crack started scribing a wide circle round the chandelier. The four diners gazed heavenward, unable to move. Then it happened with a suddenness that was shocking. The chandelier fell directly into the dining-room table with a crash followed by a cloud of plaster and the upstairs toilet, Gus still sitting on it, hands grasping his knees, bellowing. It was over in a moment. The diners gaped, hardly breathing. Slowly the toilet and Gus, teetering on a pile of rubble in the middle of the table, tipped over. All were frozen with disbelief. Then the lights on the chandelier went out.

No one spoke in the darkness. Someone whimpered. George said the first thing that came into his head: "Gus, would you like to join us for dessert in the living room?"

The last time Milton told this story, at a crowded birthday party for a mutual friend, he turned to me at the conclusion and added: "And that's exactly how the British invaded Tibet."

2.

After months of stalling and procrastinating, the Amban, the head Chinese official in Lhasa, agreed to meet with Colonel Younghusband in Gyantse. The Dalai Lama had sent a number of deputations to meet the expedition, including one depon, or general, who was sufficiently important to be clad in rich furs and have his seat carried about with him when he dismounted. That was in Tuna. Other lamas and generals had ridden out from Lhasa, always with the same message from the Dalai Lama: We will speak with you only when you agree to leave Tibet.

It was too late for that, Colonel Younghusband explained, with immense patience, always. Whatever envoy had been sent listened with immense patience of his own, then repeated what he had just said, as if the British leader had not quite understood.

While the Chinese amban, Yu-t'ai was his name, had more sympathy for the British, he too could only repeat the Dalai Lama's message, his long moustache drooping over the corners of his mouth. After all, his power in Lhasa was partly ceremonial and traditional — Peking was a long way off. He did warn Younghusband, however, that the Tibetans would try to make a stand at Gyantse.

The Amban accepted an invitation to eat with the colonel and, as they rode the short distance to the mission in the willow glade by the river, the bagpipes of the 8th Gurkhas played "Barren Rocks of Aden," the strange wailing sound echoing across the valley, up the narrow streets of the town and throughout the warren of empty rooms in Gyantse Fort, which overlooked them from its height like a stone-grey vulture.

A number of townspeople came scurrying out of nearby houses in a terrible fright, holding their ears. They gaped at the pipers pumping their sheep stomachs and puffing their cheeks. The British and Indian soldiers too responded to the call, as did Candler and his manservant. Sarge gazed, his eyes intent on the pipers.

Candler explained: "A musical instrument of our own mountain people back home. The Scots. I can see you enjoy it."

Sarge nodded, still entranced.

Candler continued, "I've always found something sad in its wail."

"Very lonely, very beautiful," Sarge said, without taking his eyes from the puffing Gurkhas.

"I guess this is the first time Tibet has heard the sound of bagpipes."

"Never forget," Sarge whispered, "never."

3.

Veronica, Edmund Candler's wife, was a woman in her mid-twenties, energetic and intelligent. She and Edmund had been married only a short while before he announced he was being asked by his paper, the *London Daily Mail*, to become their Central Asian correspondent. He readily agreed, thinking if the posting lasted more than a year, he would send for his young wife and set her up in a small house in Simla. As it turned out, the year was almost up and he barely had had time to write. All he could remember of her was the name. "Veronica" — it became everything for him that Tibet was not — England and home, the smell of warm damp earth, garden violets, softness.

Each day, Veronica consulted the *Daily Mail*, waiting and longing for news. Every day through January brought word of the impending war between Russia and Japan. While she realized Tibet was far from the hostilities, which she read finally began in early February, she knew the papers were saying Russia had a hand in the Tibetan crisis and she wondered if it would touch her Edmund.

She remembered reading her first report on Tibet the previous June. They had spelled it "Thibet" then and by November had changed to Tibet. She wondered why. But those early reports were from another correspondent in Simla. She didn't see Edmund's name on a Tibetan report, from someplace called Chumbi, until January 13.

One day, in early March, she scanned the articles on page five of the newspaper — always page five for the international news.

No report today. The weather... more rain, all summer it rained, record-breaking rains, they said, and again in February, never saw anything like it, rain rain rain, out the window, grey mounting, a few drizzles... strange, always felt something meant by rain. Fertility? Change? New ideas? Rain reflecting what's going on in the world... wonder if it rains in Tibet or Thibet? Lost *h*, where did it go? Never enough news of him, that hurts. Rain in me too... only snows in Tibet? Must have spring, flowers, sometime? But rain here all the time. Edmund wrote that there's something completely different there, a different... perception, from up high I guess, top of the world, maybe they send the rain from up there... funny, as if some cloud were broken open by British penetration, so it rains here in London... strange thoughts, what's this?

Glancing at an article that caught her eye, she read that the Dreyfus appeal was being heard in France. Poor man, she thought, poor Jew. Then she read several other articles and sipped her tea. After a while, she looked out the window and saw the rain starting to fall harder, splattering the glass. In the distance, a horse and carriage was moving away, another coming towards her.

4.

April 24, 1904   *Gyantse*

I feel I am living in a dream. When Sarge and I talk I feel as if my mind is being washed over by an irresistible wave. We take long walks in silence and yet I feel something is still being communicated. I hear his voice in my sleep. Something is burning up inside me and I do not regret its loss and yet I try to cling to what have become burning coals inside me. My skin feels like the sandpaper coat of a lizard and I long to crawl out of it.

The others too are living a dream but they fight it every moment. I pity them. I pity their stubbornness and their blindness, the pain they don't even notice.

The wrapped package continues to call to me. It is all I can do to keep from opening it. Sometimes its call is like a song, a bittersweet song of longing and sadness. It comes and goes away, comes and goes away. I let it come and go away. I feel as if a stone is being turned into a cloud, or is it my mind losing its hardness?

5.

"I dreamt my father died," Milton announced through a crust of bread as we waited for our meal in an intimate

French restaurant, a converted farmhouse, in the countryside north of Montreal.

"When?"

"This morning. Do you ever think of death, Alex?"

It wasn't the kind of discussion I relished having over a fine French dinner. We seemed to be surrounded by lovers.

"Yes, of course," I replied. "Especially when drinking red wine."

"In *vino veritas*."

"I mean it, Milton. The truth always seems to come out when I drink red wine." I took another sip of the 1982 St-Julien Milton had splurged on.

Our appetizers arrived, my soup, his lobster bits with artichokes, lemon and basil. Soup, I thought, is a misnomer.

"So many kinds of soup," I began. "Oxtail, lobster bisque, bean with bacon."

"Campbell's vegetable, Habitant pea, clam chowder," Milton took up the refrain in threes.

"Old-fashioned tomato, vichyssoise, minestrone," I chimed.

Milton raised his eyebrows in admiration: "Alphabet, French onion, matzo ball."

"International Big Bowl," I profferred, naming a popular soup at our local deli, "duck soup, chilled cucumber with sour cream."

"Ah," he chided, "no inventing recipes as we go, only real soups will be admitted to this lexical exercise."

"And this," I raised my spoon, "a hint of the taste of corn with cream and cucumber, a dollop of sour cream, finished off with a landscape designer's hedge of chopped parsley, like those old farmers' fields fenced with the stubble of tree roots wrenched from the earth."

"Fields of corn," Milton suggested.

"Of course," I slurped.

"Every culture has soup," Milton announced, as if it were one of the more basic laws of anthropology.

"Tibetan soup?" I asked.

He shrugged. "Yak brain?"

"Ah," I remembered, "nettles. Nettle soup. Milarepa, Tibet's great poet, lived on it for years. Turned his skin a strange shade of green."

"Yum," Milton commented. Raising his glass, he suggested, "Let's see if we can't turn our skin pink tonight."

We drank and ate in silence for a few moments. Then Milton began to hum. I didn't catch it at first but then realized, of course: "Soup, soup, beautiful soup..."

"Lewis Carroll, right?" He nodded. Leaning forward, he looked me in the eye and said, as the waiter began to clear the plates, "Can we get back to death?"

The waiter gave him a strange look. "Sure," I said.

"Every culture has death," he announced. "Death is like invading Tibet, getting lost in snow mountains, stark naked. Same as enlightenment. Stark naked in snow mountains, loving it." He smiled broadly, almost foolishly, and began to chuckle to himself.

Soon our dinners arrived, served with a flourish, a peach-coloured cloth napkin over the waiter's arm. I had duck in a Grand Marnier sauce, Milton had salmon stuffed with a scallop soufflé. We talked of innumerable things, growing pleasantly pinker as the meal progressed. Pink as snow ranges at dawn.

6.

At dawn, in the uncanny pink light that lasted only a moment and then was gone into yellow, then grey, the Tibetans attacked. A couple of ancient jingals began bombarding the cluster of blockhouses by the river that served as expedition headquarters. At the same moment, several hundred Tibetan soldiers rushed madly across the compound to fire their decrepit rifles in the windows at the waking British and Indians. The first attack was quickly repelled but not without the loss of a dozen Gurkhas and several British officers.

The yard was strewn with Tibetans, some still moaning, when Candler took the chance to glance out.

"They must have occupied the fort during the night," he said to Sarge across the room, sitting on the floor, his back against the wall.

Lieutenant Bailey stuck his head in the doorway, his sandy hair uncombed. "Everyone all right in here?"

"Yes, yes," Candler said. "Fine. And you?"

"I'm all right but we've got a number of injured and some finished off too. We're not quite boxed in, but they've got an excellent view of us from the jong," he said, approaching the window with care. "Colonel Ottley wants to take a party up there to blast their way in and rout them from the fort. I think he's crazy."

"He's a brave soldier," Sarge said seriously.

"And a fool," added Candler;.

"That too," said Bailey.

As it turned out, the fresh Tibetan troops who had arrived from distant Kham in the eastern part of the country were not all that easy to dislodge from the fort. Ottley was not able to rout them, since they had fortified the jong on their arrival. From their position overlooking the town they rained cannon shot down on the expedition forces. For the next few days, the troops in the mission were busy building traverses to protect against the shelling. While the fort also afforded a good view of the surrounding countryside, the expedition was able to keep its supply line in shape so the troops never lacked for food, water or even the post, which came on an irregular basis. They settled in for a long wait, knowing that fresh British and Indian troops on their way from Darjeeling would be needed to overwhelm the hundreds of Tibetans defending the jong.

7.

Three weeks they waited, sending out patrols in the dead of night to clear and secure nearby houses and to terrorize the enemy. Sarge and Candler spent the time helping to fortify the mission with heavy cross-beams, talking, reading and trying to stay out of harm's way. Candler sensed that they were resting up for the final push to Lhasa. He also felt that it was the calm before the storm, in more ways than one.

In early July the long column of new troops arrived, complete with pack animals and coolies loaded down with new supplies. Several Tibetan attempts to stop them on the way had failed. Two days later, the expeditionary forces directed an all-out attack at the jong. After blasting a hole with cannon shot and gun-cotton in the three-foot-thick wall, Gurkhas led by British officers poured through and routed the Tibetan troops from the fort with a great loss of life and much suffering. By late afternoon, it was over. The remaining Tibetans fled, abandoning Gyantse to the British.

That evening, Candler went down by the river with its soft willows dragging their yellow-green limbs in the water. He washed the blood from his one good hand. For hours he had been helping, as well as he could, haul the dead and wounded, expeditionary forces and Tibetans alike, either to large open graves or to a hastily assembled camp hospital. The operating table on which he had written his dispatches had been commandeered and put to its proper use.

Resting on the ground, he watched the water flow by. After gazing for a while, he turned and looked up at the men still working in the half-light behind him. The motion of the water lingered in his eyes, causing the men to swim in his vision as if they too were flowing away. He looked at his hand again. The air around him was blood red.

8.

High atop the jong, a Union Jack flapped among the prayer flags, tattered remnants of cloth eaten by weather, whatever colour they once held leached by rain, snow and sun. For now, however, Candler watched them whipping together in the wind, all pointing the same direction — towards Lhasa.

Soon the force would leave Gyantse and head up the rough road leading to the capital. Candler surmised that it would be easy going from here — it seemed the Tibetans had made their toughest stand yet and it had amounted to little more than a few weeks' delay. Still, it was rough country and the rare air alone took its toll on both men and animals.

Candler thought he would miss Gyantse, at least the cluster of willows by the river where he felt most strongly the peace that held this land. Strange business, he thought, I feel as if I too am being invaded, in a gentle, subtle way, but all the more profound and unforgettable for that. Like the songs of the vegetable hawkers in the back alleys of Delhi — he could hear that song wherever he went, as if it were welling up in his own chest, a sound he didn't hear with his ears but with his heart and with his own lungs as they echoed the breathing rhythm of the singer, unconsciously, yet, in the same way, the river and the willows, rasping quietly in the breeze also rose up inside him and joined with something else...what was it? And then he heard it, yes, yes, that's it..."Candler," Sarge said, standing behind him.

9.

Milton and I were having coffee at Dunn's Deli. Snow was falling again, beyond the stacked jars of pickles in the window. Cars sliced through slush and splattered salt. Kali Yuga.

Milton turned from the window, sipped his coffee. "Have you found all the info you need on Candler?" he asked.

"I've got the outer story, if you know what I mean," I answered, holding a spoon poised over my cup, "but what I need now is the inner story, maybe even the secret story. I might have to go away to get those."

Milton nodded. "Where did we leave off?"

"When Macdonald got to Gyantse with his fresh troops," I continued, "he was ill again and had to be carried in a doolie when the column moved out for Lhasa about three weeks later."

Younghusband sat on his horse and looked down at his military commander. "What's wrong with you?" he asked.

Macdonald coughed, averted his eyes. "Don't know. Weak. Head feels like it's splitting open."

"Altitude," Younghusband concluded and rode off for the head of the column, not prescribing a remedy, for there wasn't one that he knew of.

Later, in the early evening after setting up camp in the lee of a mountain to the north, Sarge took green herbs from a cloth bag, mixed them with hot tea and gave some to Macdonald as well as several other men who had complained of headache.

Macdonald drank, high bald forehead sweating. Sarge watched like a cat as Macdonald's eyes never stopped moving, searching the peaks, straining into the whelming dark.

"What are you afraid of?" Sarge asked.

Macdonald, on the *doolie* in front of his tent, looked away, towards an outcropping of rock. "Nothing," he replied. Candler, sitting on a camp-stool, watched.

"This?" Sarge asked, holding out his hand.

Candler saw that it contained a half-dozen pieces of bone: knucklebones, fingerbones, a vertebra.

Macdonald looked. "No, not that. I am afraid of nothing."

Candler noticed that Sarge had not expected this answer. The Tibetan gave Macdonald a long look, one that was as hard as ice yet banked with the fires of compassion.

10.

The next day Sarge and Candler rode side by side, near the column's rear. The country was empty, a wind always blowing.

"When you were in India, did you visit a place called Rajgir?" Sarge asked.

"Yes, in fact, I did," Candler said. "I had befriended a young Indian man from Bombay. We took several journeys together. He was well-educated, spoke English and was of invaluable assistance to me. Once we passed near this place, Rajgir, and he insisted we visit.

He had told me he was a Buddhist and that this mountain spot was a place where the Buddha himself had taught. As we climbed up he went on and on about how wonderful it was to be able to visit this holy place — he had been there several times before, you see — describing in great detail how powerful it was to experience such a spot. When we finally reached Rajgir, I looked out at the folds of mountains rippling away into the distance and I felt nothing, nothing at all, not a thing."

Sarge nodded, "You understood perfectly." And then it seemed Sarge wanted to say no more so they rode on in silence.

11.

Although it was now early summer, the high pass the column had traversed had a sheer wall of stone running parallel with the men on their southern flank. Its shadow kept the pass in its grip for miles. Little grew there but tufts of grass, like hair on the heads of donkeys. The force made camp early. Once Sarge and Candler had set up their tent, they rode off to explore the area.

As they rounded a bend, Sarge took off on his pony with the white blaze on its forehead. "Follow me!" he shouted.

After a hard ride of twenty minutes, the two riders passed through a narrow defile and came into a high pasture open to the south. It was waving sensuously with grass and wildflowers. Candler was shocked with the green as it struck his eyes. It glowed with evening sunlight. He quickly counted at least ten rhododendrons of variously coloured blossoms, including some of the loveliest pale primrose yellow among the pines at the field's edge. The ground was carpeted with flowers. Primulas, gentians, anemones, celandines, wild strawberries, irises. The colours filled his eyes like nectar: sulphur yellows, shiny berry red, waxy purple, pure whites and a thousand shades of green. The sky fell towards dusk with a deepening soft blue that made it look as if it were melting into water. The facets of the surrounding snow-capped peaks lit up with the most amazing array of brilliant shimmering pinks and golds.

Suddenly, on a large flat rock ahead of him, Candler saw Sarge, dismounted, facing away from him. He had a huge sword in his hand shining with a diamond-clear light — at times appearing as if it weren't there at all. Sarge was swinging the sword which now seemed to be in flames — or was it just the way it was catching the light?

Candler watched as Sarge turned around — for a moment it didn't appear to be Sarge at all. He was dressed in brilliant armour, his face glowing. His eyes were black and shining, all black, no white to be seen.

They seemed empty and full at the same time. Completely empty. Completely full.

12.

Candler noticed, almost without noticing, that the small wrapped Buddha more and more began to prey on his mind. The powerful urge to open it seldom left him. But somehow he sensed that he should try to forget about it, let go of it.

Gold! Perhaps it is a statue of pure gold or a huge jewel — a diamond or ruby. I could lose it and never know what's inside! Or perhaps it is a magic crystal, one of those milky white stones about which I have read — all the world revealed in them, past and future, everything. I would have immense power.

Then a peculiar thought came to him: Perhaps it's not a statue at all but my own hand. The one blown off and left lying in a stony field. Perhaps it is some kind of joke that Tibetan girl is playing on me.

Going to his trunk, he lifted the lid and rummaged about for the package. It was in his hand, as heavy as ever, the strings wrapped in criss-cross patterns. What, what is it? he wondered. Ever since they had left Gyantse, the journey had been like a shimmering dream. Perhaps it has something to do with this statue. He weighed it. "Mystery. Mystery it is and mystery it shall remain," he whispered, placing it back in the bottom of his trunk.

Perhaps it's the altitude, he thought, holding his head. But everything seems so strange. The colours of the mountains go vivid with minor shiftings of the light; it's uncanny, unreal. And Macdonald grows more and more ill. The men whisper now that he is dying, but no one mentions it out loud. And Sarge seems to gain in some mysterious way, to grow in power, to become more and more... inscrutable. It feels now not as if we are a conquering army, but as if we are being drawn into something, slipping down a long slope into a lake of illimitable depth, while everything grows brighter, brighter.

CHAPTER VIII

———— ✦ ————

1.

"What we need here, I believe, is for the gods to send down a false dream, yes, that's it, a false dream." The double-decker bus roared and swayed through a long, warm afternoon. I was alone on the second level of the bus, except for an unusual-looking couple sitting several seats ahead of me. There was a distinguished-looking elderly man, obviously blind. I had noticed his milky-white eyes gazing off blankly towards the ceiling when I boarded. He was listening to a beautiful young woman read from a manuscript.

I forget where I was headed that day, but it was obvious to me that the couple in front was headed nowhere in particular. They were immersed in their reading and discussion. She read beautifully, with a soft, mellifluous voice that carried well. I couldn't help but listen in.

"The other gods and all the fighting men slept through the night, but there was no easeful sleep for Zeus." She would read a few lines and then he would comment. "Yes, a false dream," he said, "we must send them a false dream," and she would make a few changes in the manuscript.

Of course, it was the second chapter of the *Iliad*, in which we learn that the Trojans have been fated to lose the war. How strange, I thought, looking out the window. On this dreamy summer afternoon, drifting through the streets of London, it appears as if the two of them are writing the book for the first time. No, this is no new translation — something bizarre and other-wordly took hold of me — no, they are actually playing out the original tale! Up here on the second level of a bus, looking down on the swirling city, as if not part of it at all, as if separate from its chaos and desires and fears, removed as the gods are removed and working out the fates of little men. My head began to swirl and I grew dizzy. When I opened my eyes, the top of her head was disappearing down the spiral stairs. They were gone.

2.

A dream is a living thing, whether false or true. The ancients knew that. I was about to learn it. The last words I heard from the blind man on the bus were: "The dream listened, then set forth on its errand..." The girl bowed her head, wrote it down. Our dreams speak to us each night, but seldom do they listen. This takes a kind of power, to make a dream listen. This power is one about which I know little — only that it exists.

Several days later, I took an afternoon nap, which I seldom do. At one point, I thought I had awakened...I'm not sure still if I was awake or asleep dreaming I had awakened. At any rate, Auntie Liz stood at the foot of my bed, looking ghostly, surrounded by a ghost kitchen: a portion of kitchen counter, her small stove, part of her refrigerator. She was wearing an apron and holding a frying pan. But there was something odd about it — she held the frying pan upside-down and was peering into the back of it, the way Tibetans will look into metal mirrors to foresee the future.

"What do you see?" I asked.

"Shhh!" She hushed me, waving her free hand in my direction. "The walls of the city are trembling. I hear strange music. Let's see now. There's Edmund Candler. And there's a Tibetan fellow with him. Handsome devil." She winked in my direction. "Oh, this is bad, very bad." She had resumed her gazing. "Hmm. I suggest you drop this Tibetan business

immediately, Alex. It's going to lead you to plenty
of grief. Forget it. Do something worthwhile, like
Arnold does. He helps people. He's a doctor, though
god knows, Alex, I hold no brief for doctors. But
at least he tries." Her face had taken on a purple hue
and she was grimacing at me. She looked almost
demonic as her voice changed into a hysterical shriek,
high-pitched and wailing. "I'm warning you," she was
almost screaming now, "forget this bad business!
Forget Candler and Tibet! Leave it!" Something within
me stiffened, once I had gotten over the initial shock
at the change in her demeanour.

"No, I won't leave it," I said simply and without
anger. "No, I'm going to continue...all the way to
Lhasa with Candler and Sarge and I'm going to find
out what this expedition is really about."

She softened and smiled, and there was something
in her look that I had seen in a photograph of Sarge
(Candler had asked Lieutenant Bailey to take it on
their arrival in Lhasa), some subtle glance or shining
on the cheekbones. "I'm glad. I was just testing you.
Good luck, Alex. Take care of yourself. Farewell."
And she was gone.

I think I awoke for a second time, my eyes, already
open, opened again.

Something in me sensed that she was gone, really
gone, for good. Along with her went my last direct
link to Candler. And then an odd thought struck me:
Perhaps she was the only thing separating me from
Candler, keeping me stuck in a traditional perception
of time. Perhaps now I could truly go into Candler's

head, as if our times had melded or as if mistaken notions of time could be dropped at last. How strange that the one thing connecting me to him was also the one thing keeping me separate from him. When I heard in the evening that Auntie Liz had indeed died that very morning, I felt that I would be connected to Candler again, but in a completely different way, and although I was profoundly saddened, I felt nothing but gratitude to Auntie Liz for making it possible.

3.

July 16, 1904   Between Ralung and Karo La

Am I alone mad? Or has the entire world gone insane? I have only questions now, no answers to soothe my fever. I look at Sarge, I look at the others, I look at the great abyss between them, the abyss I am attempting to span — and I am being torn in two by the effort. What are we doing here? What!? Such idiocy.

I am put in this position by what I have seen: either I am mad or all the others are mad and I alone am sane. Henry Newman came up to me yesterday in the mess, the man is forever pulling contentedly on his pipe. "Pull yourself together," he said. "You look as if you just saw a ghost, as if you're flying apart." Yes, flying apart, from a stone into a cloud — I am that package, that bound figure about to explode. I'm bursting apart...

What has brought me to this? Sarge's words? His presence, overwhelming in its power? My own thoughts riddled with confusion and longing? This land itself with its excruciating heights and clarity? Why do the others not see it? Why am I alone fated to see it?

Tomorrow we cross the Karo La — the scouts tell us the pass is over sixteen thousand feet. We are surrounded by high summer now. Both the rare air and the beauty here take my breath away. I will go out into the night ringing with cold clear stars, a Ghurka's kukri sword of moon will slice off my head and I will think, at last, of nothing.

4.

Between Gubchi and Ralung the troops had passed houses decorated with diagonal stripes of blue, red and white, a sign of the Ning-ma sect of Buddhists. Heavy rains slowed the advance.

The next day the expedition camped in a sodden mustard field and, in the morning, began the gradual ascent to the Karo Pass. Four miles from the pass they camped again, expecting that the Karo would be heavily defended. A majestic glacier ended five hundred feet from the camp.

In the mess, the men discussed the next day's movements. The Gurkhas, sturdy Indians familiar with the mountains, were most acclimated to the heights and would thus bear the brunt of the climbing and fighting. The walls of the narrow pass would undoubtedly have to be cleared of Tibetan riflemen before the main body of troops could move up to attack the forces behind the loose-stone sangar built across the bottom of the pass.

The next morning, Candler and Sarge sat in sunshine on a grassy knoll some distance from the fighting and watched through binoculars as scaling parties of Gurkhas climbed the heights. The rapping of Maxim guns could be heard as well as the boom of the ten-pounders which echoed down the valley. The Gurkhas could be seen routing armed Tibetans from high shelves and shallow caves. The usual slaughter ensued and the Tibetans fled, not even bothering to defend the position behind the sangar.

Candler watched as a handful of Gurkhas stood before a larger cave mouth high up the cliff. They looked oddly out of place with their high tight boots and their wide-brimmed soft hats turned up on the left side. One of them leaned and looked in and was immediately shot, falling over backwards. A Tibetan came out of the cave, red cloth twined into his long hair showing him to be a man of Kham, threw down his rifle and begged for mercy. Three Gurkhas leapt forward, slicing him into pieces with their kukris. Dragging four more Tibetans out of the cave, they threw them off the cliff three hundred feet to their deaths. It was like a dream, Candler thought, watching those men fall through the air. He turned to look at Sarge, whose expression was blank. Candler sighed, looked again at the cliffside, scanned down the lower reaches of the pass. There he saw Ottley riding hard after an unarmed Tibetan, also a Khampa, who was trying to flee. Ottley's sword flashed in the morning light and the man's head, red braid unravelling, went flying off and rolled down into a gulley. The strange-looking trunk stood a moment, then pitched forward.

Another light flashed from high up the cliffside — the Gurkhas heliographed that the Tibetans were defeated and the pass was clear.

As they followed the troops through the pass, Candler noticed that Sarge kept leaning off his pony to search the roadside. At last, he leapt down and shouted for Candler to follow. Skittering down a small gravel hill, Candler watched Sarge reach among a cluster of boulders and pick up, by the hair, the head of the man Ottley had cut down. Candler recoiled from the sight, blood still oozing from the severed neck. "Look at it," Sarge demanded.

The man's open eyes gazed out blankly. He looks familiar, thought Candler. Remove the red braid and

138

the long hair and there is a face I have seen before
. . . where? Suddenly the realization struck Candler.
His breath caught and an uncontrollable mad scream
burst from his lungs. Scrambling back up the hill,
he heard Sarge coming behind, laughing. Candler
wondered why it had taken him so long to recognize
his own face.

Remounting his pony, Sarge handed Candler the
red cloth. As Candler took it from him, Sarge clasped
his hand and squeezed. "Courage," Sarge whispered.
Candler broke down and wept.

5.

The background sound of the engine hummed a
droning accompaniment to our conversation as Milton
and I drove the expressway from Montreal to Ottawa,
a journey of some two hours. Milton wanted to find
a certain commentary on the Kabbala that apparently
existed only at the National Library, while I came along
for the ride. At that time, Milton was driving an old,
failing Rover T-2000, not a Land Rover but the sporty
sedan type with leather seats and toggle switches on
the dashboard. The Rover, he explained, was an
automobile "designed and built by idiots for sale to
fools. British, you know, quite useless." And yet I

knew he loved the beast, despite the fact that the cost of repairs on it was keeping the families of three Jamaican mechanics happy and well-fed.

"For god's sake, Alex." (We were discussing, among other things, magic — this subject coming out of his interest in the Kabbala — and he was growing quite lathered, beginning to show a touch of the lambent bitterness which sometimes surfaced in him, with some justification, I must add.) "For god's sake, most people wouldn't know magic if it clubbed them in the head, most people are dead asleep, walking corpses, Alex, so stunned and depleted by trivial facts, blinding desires and stupefying fears that they can accomplish their basic survival habits and that's it. They're deeply afraid of the magic that is constantly welling up in their lives, turning their faces from it, because if they looked at it they might have to see that things are not quite what they seem. I'm not talking about rabbits in hats, either, or even paranormal bullshit. I mean, for god's sake, here we are sitting in a goddamn living room roaring down the highway at seventy miles an hour and we're so inured to it that we can't even feel the bizarreness of that. We're stunned — you and me too, for the most part. But at least we're willing to try to take a look at that and see why."

We were passed on the highway by a Wonder Bread truck, the familiar red, blue and yellow polka dots drifting by us at seventy-five miles per hour. I pointed and we both laughed.

"You know," he continued, "magic is the same as art, at its root, and the ultimate art is to be lucid without straining. And I mean lucid in all its senses. Not only clear, but shining, brilliant, sane. If you have that state of mind, then you see magic everywhere, every moment. If people would sit down and look, just stop and sit for a while, the world would be a much better place."

"Sounds like the prescription of the Tibetan meditators," I suggested.

"Sure, sitting till they get calluses on their butts like old Milarepa. But it's not a big deal, either. We have to remember irony, at all times. Magic, well, it's the rain and snow falling, the wind, eating dinner...Damn, I wish I had a pickle. But you know what I mean. Magic is so utterly ordinary it's just the world as it is, as it really is, without need of our recommendations, suggestions or additions."

I placed my hand on the dashboard. "Somebody told me once that the automobile would one day be considered a momentary aberration in the history of technology, somewhat in the same way that we consider the blimp today. That kind of thinking is magic, because it makes you see the absurdity of your situation. And, of course, the existentialists might get quite depressed about the seeming absurdity of our lives while Zen and other Buddhists would look at that same fact and find it humorous. It's actually quite delightful when you think of it — hurtling down the highway while sitting in what amounts to a living room."

"Bizarre too," Milton added. We both felt for a moment totally displaced...in the car and not in the car at the same time, seeing ourselves in a situation that was familiar yet new.

The usual response to this feeling, I thought, is to say something about it, continue the conversation, come to a neat conclusion, always this need to square things off at the end, but we were talked out and, as always, we were left with silence, our own silence, either haunted by it or comfortable with it, depending on our own states of mind, our moods, our particular habitual patterns. I looked at Milton. He was driving, just driving, his face glowing with pure enjoyment.

6.

On Tuesday, July 7, 1904, Veronica sat in London reading her *Daily Mail*. She noticed a dispatch from Simla:

WEIRD STORY FROM BURMA
(From Our Own Correspondent)
Simla, Thursday, June 18

A story comes from Burma of a six-year-old Burmese boy in the Pegu district who is believed by the simple villagers around him to be the reincarnation of the late Mr. A.H. Tucker, district superintendent of police, who was killed by dacoits in 1894.

The child has been taken to various places where Mr. Tucker was stationed, and the Burmese declare that he remembers all the incidents of his previous existence. At the place of the murder he trembled and gave particulars of the deed, they say, and nothing will persuade them that the spirit of the late Mr. Tucker has not returned to earth in the shape of the boy.

Such reincarnation is generally believed in Burma, and numerous alleged examples of it are on record. The reincarnated ones are called "*winzas.*"

At the same moment, or one much like it, I, Alex, sat one kilometer to the east, at my familiar seat in the British Library, reading an account by Candler of a strange old woman that he and Sarge had met several days' ride from Lhasa. It was not what the old woman said or did that set me to trembling. Rather, it was Candler's description of her and his attitude towards her. I felt certain that the old woman was Auntie Liz reincarnated. I looked up from the book. No, that's not right...I'm reading of the past...how is it I've...hmmm...I must have confused the time...times...Looking down, the words began swimming on the page, rearranging themselves into new patterns, but always the same old words, same letters...the book was pulsing in my hands or was I feeling my own pulse shooting down my arms and out to my fingertips making it only appear as if the book itself were alive? Well, I am alive, why couldn't the book be alive?

And then, one of the young clerks who delivered books to the seats, was pulling me by the arm and saying: "Are you all right, sir? I believe you've fainted. It is warm in here today."

The clerk gave me a strange look when I replied: "No, no...it's the altitude...I'll be fine...fine."

7.

Candler gazed at the muscle in Younghusband's jaw. He could see it tensing. That was the point where Younghusband's frustrations at the length of this needless journey found their focus, the point where the fears and broken hopes collected and hardened in his body. Candler imagined what his skull might look like, imagined that point where the lower jaw was hinged, pictured the colonel's head in its essence. Bone, like these denuded mountains, like these people with their basic, simple lives of eating and talking. The higher they climbed in this journey, the more basic life became. The food at the mess became plainer and plainer. The supply line now was hundreds of miles long through some of the most treacherous landscape in the world. Letters were few and far between. The stringing of the telegraph cables was taking longer than expected. They saw few people, few animals. During the past several days of marching they had not even seen any vegetation, other than a sprinkling of grey lichen. Everywhere rock. Even the moon that night, a week shy of full, seemed stone. The raw daylight was powdered stone. The horses were sculpted of granite, tensed, muscular, hard. Candler watched the clenching of Younghusband's jaw.

"We are nearing Lhasa," the colonel announced to the assembled officers and a few others. He stopped. All waited for him to say something, but he seemed to have lost the thread or the reason for calling the meeting. "We are nearing Lhasa..." He stopped again, his large grey-blue eyes gazing at the floor, unable to go on. "The mountains seem to have affected my ability to think." The assembled men nodded, accepting this explanation. More long silences followed. It appeared that there was no real purpose for the meeting. A few details were discussed but everyone seemed fatigued and eventually the officers started to drift off one by one.

Candler found it all very strange, especially when he looked out the commander's tent and saw Sarge nearby, grinning, almost glowing with delight.

Later Candler asked him, "What happened there? What is happening? A malaise seems to have struck everyone." Sarge was still beaming.

"The mountains are having their effect. You see the world as stone, but there is more than stone here.

There is much space in the mountains. It invades the mind. There is nothing to think about up here. Too bad you cannot relax. Too bad the mountains depress you English so all you can see is the stone, the rockiness of it, the hardness. You don't understand. You don't see. It's wonderful. I feel like I could throw the mountains about they are so light, full of space, empty. Hah, hah!"

He bounded away from the tents, his high leather boots flying over the broken ground.

Later, when he returned, Sarge said, "Don't get me wrong. I like you English. Something in the British mind is quite strong and loyal. But it is too bad you English are so fond of death, and yet afraid of it." A quizzical look crossed his face.

8.

Sarge and Candler stood over a narrow crevice staring down.

"Do you see it now?" Sarge asked.

"Yes...why yes I do!" Candler was astonished.

About six feet down inside the crevice, on a shelf of stone, was a book, a small Tibetan-style book, that is to say long and narrow, with a wooden cover. It had been placed so as to be protected from the weather and looked to be in decent repair, at least from this distance. But...what was a book doing here, in this wasteland? Sarge and Candler had been out for a walk near the encampment. Colonel Younghusband had called a halt of several days to allow the supply lines to catch up. Time weighed on the men in the empty mountains. There were few animals to shoot at, no residents, not even any nomads passing through. It was sheer luck that Sarge had noticed the book in the crevice.

"Shall we take a closer look?" he asked.

Soon he was holding Candler by the ankles as the journalist slid upside-down along the face of the crevice, edging towards the book. Candler was hauled out clutching it in his one good hand.

"How strange," he mumbled, gazing at it. They sat down next to each other, Candler holding the book in his lap, turning the pages with care.

"Very ancient *terma*," commented Sarge. "The script, it is Tibetan but I do not recognize all of it. I shall have to examine it more carefully."

"*Terma?*" Candler questioned.

"Yes. Secret books hidden in the earth by great teachers. Or sometimes secret teachings planted in the minds of people to be realized at some time in the future. Let me see."

Later, they sat in Candler's tent discussing what Sarge had learned of the book after reading it earnestly for several hours.

"It speaks of mountains, that is all. It says that the mountains are not external phenomena but inside things. Each thing, each being in the world has a mountain inside. This mountain never changes, although its colours change according to the angle of the sun and the time of year. The sun too has a mountain inside it. Our minds also have mountains inside them. There are no external mountains. They are a figment of our imaginations, no more than words on a page."

"I don't quite understand. What is the meaning of this? Are these mountains something to be conquered?"

"Conquered?" Sarge questioned. "No, I don't think so. Not mountains as the English treat the mountains of Tibet. No, no. Quite different. Nevertheless, these mountains have snow and ice on top. They are unapproachable except to the whitest of snow lions who disappear in them. Do you understand me?"

"No," said Candler.

"You will," said Sarge.

CHAPTER IX

—————•————

1.

Milton's past was as ambiguous as his present. I could never decide if the past he related to me was the one he had experienced or the one he had imagined. After some time, the idea dawned on me that perhaps there wasn't any difference, at least not in Milton's mind, the only place, after all, where his own personal past existed.

When Milton was a child he had taken piano lessons from a woman named Madame Bauhaud, a kindly intelligent woman from the border country between France and Italy. After several years of lessons, Milton's family began to treat Madame Bauhaud as a friend. It was then they learned that she was actually a noblewoman down on her luck. Her father had been royalty in some obscure house or other and then had fallen on hard times due to a catastrophe the nature of which was difficult to discern, even for Madame Bauhaud. It could have been political or economic or religious. Milton suspected a sexual scandal of some sort.

He explained, late one evening in his apartment as we relaxed over glasses of Calvados, that Madame Bauhaud had remained a friend of the Kasma family long after Milton had rebelled at piano lessons. She was a dignified, tall woman of indeterminate age and, as they learned, a master of eight languages with an abiding interest in world literature. Milton recalled her long thin fingers most clearly, and her delicate, expressive hands which seemed to speak a language all their own.

Eventually, Madame Bauhaud moved to Italy. She had inherited a villa there, complete with its own servants, livestock and vineyards. Located in central Italy on the route between Perugia and Assisi, at the foot of a high hill, the villa was a stately affair with grand rooms and ancient wine cellars. Despite the relocation, Madame Bauhaud wrote faithfully to Milton's mother, who never suspected that the escape from Canada allowed Madame Bauhaud to give vent to her latent eccentricities. When Milton began travelling, in his early twenties, it was only natural that he stop in to visit Madame Bauhaud on his way from Milan to Rome. Planning to stay two days, he stayed three weeks.

A sliver of moon could be seen slicing across the window of Milton's apartment. The evening traffic was dying down. We were entering that part of the day when time loses its foothold, when the hours slip by without notice. His voice, the Calvados, the late hour all conspired to charm me into a blessed reverie at the edge of narcosis. "What made you stay?" I asked. "Please go on." Of course, he had never had any intention of stopping, but I thought I would encourage him in conjuring this momentary state of blissful contemplation.

He stared into the small grate in his living room. "Let's make a fire," he said, jumping up. It was mid-November, a fire was justified, barely. As he built and lit it, I watched and waited. We said nothing. Once the fire had begun to breathe steadily, he resumed his seat. A fire, I thought, is always a perfect reflection of one's psychological state. If it starts badly and is troubled, that says something about the situation at hand. In this case, I noted that the fire leapt into full strength without a pause. It had no dangerous infancy, no troubled youth. But the fire was not crazed, certainly not maniacal. It pumped steadily, avoiding any suggestion of lethargy. It glowed.

Milton gazed into the fire and spoke and I realized that he had wanted the fire to look at, the better to clarify his memories in the crucible. He explained that Madame Bauhaud had answered the door of the villa herself, a three-foot iguana on her shoulder (two feet of tail). He knew this was not quite the same staid woman who had been his piano teacher some years earlier. The combination of great inherited wealth, which had finally come her way after the hard times, and the anonymity of being a foreigner in the land, had led to her relaxing of normal civilized codes of conduct. She did as she pleased.

Among her servants was a woman of fifty years or so, about ten years younger than Madame Bauhaud, who had become the elder woman's companion. The woman had a Pico della Mirandola mind in an Umbrian peasant's body. She possessed an intellect of uncanny brilliance, was able to recall texts and languages she had heard but once. Madame Bauhaud had taught her the eight languages she herself knew and they read to each other constantly from various literatures. They were often to be overheard conversing in Greek, Latin, Hebrew or Hungarian. Milton had no idea why Madame Bauhaud had learned Hungarian although he suspected it was done in order to read a certain text that intrigued her. Madame Bauhaud referred to the other woman as the Popess, or Guglielma.

As is often the case with those who possess wondrous or miraculous intellect, Guglielma was also capable of the most haunting displays of imbalance. The slightest unseen disturbance in the atmosphere would cause her to plummet from apparent sanity into the depths of madness. Somehow the Madame had managed to curb Guglielma's fits, to ease them into something more useful and intriguing. Instead of the usual screaming and thrashing one finds in the performances of the mad, Guglielma would tumble through the vast encyclopedic reaches of her mind and come out with random quotes, well-stated, clear, not too histrionic but announced with enough fervour to be always of interest to the listener.

Many an evening, Milton explained, they sat about a huge oak table strewn with books, arcane texts, volumes long lost to the world, all drawn from the villa's enormous library which was said to have one of the best collections in Italy and was renowned in certain circles for its works on Tibet. Glasses of red wine from bottles that had lain in the cellars perfecting themselves for fifty, sixty, seventy years, also were a required presence on the table. And no matter how often they were emptied, they always seemed full.

Madame Bauhaud sat at the head of the table, erect and dignified, the iguana she had named "Piccola Salamandra" on her shoulder. Guglielma, the Popess, sat to her left while Milton sat to her right. Milton described these evenings, which often ended at dawn, as the pinnacle of his life, the high pass that led into a new world, the moment when everything changed. They were escapades into the paradisal realms of poetry and language, conversations that led from the lowest seaside jungles up into the crisp altitudes of plunging mountains.

"The excellence of the wine was no hindrance to the quality of the conversation, either," he added.

Every twenty or thirty minutes, Guglielma would have a fit, throw her head back, the whites of her eyes glowing like mountain snow, and begin to babble. For a few moments, she would blather on, making altogether no sense, although it seemed as if she were merely building up a head of steam for she would soon launch into a sensible quote from Joyce, or Beckett, or Conrad, or Lévi-Strauss, or Tang Dynasty poetry, or Melville, or a few random cantos from Pound, or an arcane Tibetan text on the Heart Sutra (once, the Heart Sutra itself, while Milton was there, in its Tibetan, Sanskrit, English and Italian versions), or a series of haiku by Bashō, or a hundred lines from Dante's *Inferno* in gorgeous mellifluous Italian, or a few humorous paragraphs from Raymond Queneau's *Le Chiendent* in which he describes a French seaside resort during vacation time, or a dip into Lawrence Durrell's reflections on Greece, or a bit of Old Testament, and once, as a striking anomaly, the entire periodic table. And on Milton's final evening at the Villa Bauhaud, this single line from Sophocles: "Do this one thing for me," which seemed as if it had been spoken by the original Antigone herself, so profound and moving was it coming from the mouth of this Italian madwoman.

Madame Bauhaud's parrot, Julius the Second, always had the last word. "Enough!" he would screech from his mahogany perch in a corner of the room, the cry never coming too soon nor too late. His vocabulary was limited (if one word can be considered a vocabulary) but his timing was exquisite.

The fire sighed in the grate, consoling, calming. Milton gazed at it continually as he spoke, never looking up but watching the flames pulse. Somewhere in the middle of a sentence, in the middle of the bottle of Calvados, in the middle of the night, I fell asleep.

2.

July 22, 1904   Pehte Jong

Something has been shattered and is drifting away. Yesterday they blew up a temple with gun-cotton. A huge bronze Buddha burning. I saw it. Whenever again I look into a fire or a flame of any kind I will see that Buddha there, burning, melting away among the ruins, flames red against blue sky. Tomorrow we reach the Tsangpo River. We draw near. Shattered. Yesterday, or was it two days ago, a *durbar*, a public audience with three Shapés, representatives of the Dalai Lama. Their servants carried large umbrellas. Nothing. Everyone speaks, no one listens. Shattered apart. Did it explode? I can't remember. Something exploded. Behind my eyes perhaps. I send no more dispatches. Something shattered. It's ironic. Younghusband's doubts. He does his duty. And I think the Tibetans admire him for it! I saw a flock of ducks yesterday taking off from a lake. Saw a tomb with a famous teacher buried there — Atisa, was it? A simple quiet place. I wanted to stay there forever. Sarge led me back. I feel like a child. Younghusband hates doing it, but he does his duty. Slaves, Sarge calls us. Slaves to what? I wonder. To habit? The past? Our own minds? Yes, that must be it. I dreamt of a salamander last night. Two stars in the Milky Way were rubbing their hands together. Was it on Yamdok Lake that I saw the ducks?

3.

Madame Bauhaud's eyes flickered over the page she was reading to Milton, her young guest, and Guglielma, the one she had dubbed the Popess. The text she held was the thirteenth volume of Aladdin and the Enchanted Lamp; Zein Ul Asnam and the King of the Jinn: two stories done into English from the recently discovered Arabic text by John Payne, Khorassan Edition, Number 406 of five hundred copies, printed for subscribers only in London in 1901. The book was dedicated to Captain Sir Richard Francis Burton, K.C.M.G., H.B.M. Consul in Trieste. She read: " 'O my lord,' rejoined the Imam, 'this is a thing exceeding hard to find; but I know a damsel unique in her loveliness and her age is fifteen years...' " She paused. "You see, Milton, young man, the damsel, the one true book, the exquisite light are all..." She was interrupted by Guglielma's chair scraping back on the marble floor. The Popess grunted deeply, threw her head back and declaimed: "Mah . . . mah . . . mahont . . . mmmahou . . . mmmahount . . . mhountain . . . mountain . . . mountain . . . mountain . . . go round . . . mountain . . . red mountain . . . blue mmountain violet . . . violet mountain . . . mountain . . . mountain we go round and round inside us we go round . . . shining light stone light diamond shining mountain diamond mountain . . . " She repeated the refrain "diamond . . . mountain . . . diamond . . . mountain . . ." for about five minutes as if the repetition itself were a way of going around and around the mountain.

Milton gazed at her throat as she said the words "diamond mountain" over and over again. There was something soothing about it; he could see the pulse in her neck, the movement as the words rose up the throat and exited from the lips, over and over, "diamond mountain . . . diamond mountain," she was saying it quietly now, more and more quietly, soothing herself with the words, until she finally stopped, brought her gaze back down to the table, placed her hands there and sighed. Madame Bauhaud covered Guglielma's rough peasant hands with her own, in a tender fashion, and smiled.

"Guglielma has just given you a taste of a text we read several weeks ago. An ancient Tibetan book which we found utterly fascinating. It spoke of the wheel and how, to the Buddhist, the wheel is symbol of both bondage and liberation. If you go around the mountain correctly, you can use the going around as a means to free yourself or you can go around the mountain incorrectly, that is, with ignorance, which will dig you deeper and deeper into bondage. You see, Milton, we think the same thoughts over and over again in our lives. Seldom does anything new enter our minds. But we can use that circling energy, that habit, we can harness it to serve another purpose. Guglielma, in her wisdom, has shown you this."

It was very late at night, or early in the morning, the cock soon to crow, though the stately windows of the room were black as ink and threw Milton back upon himself when he looked out.

"You must understand who Guglielma is, Milton. I'd like you to understand. Guglielma is the rebirth of an earlier Guglielma, the founder of the Guglielmites, a thirteenth-century Christian sect that saw the Papacy as failing in its spiritual leadership and insisted on a spiritual revitalizing of religious life. She made some mistakes. For one, she saw herself as the third person of the Trinity, the Holy Spirit, and for that sin of pride she now suffers her madness, her possessions, which I have helped her to bear. For another, she appointed Manfreda as the Popess when she should have appointed herself. Things would have gone much better for her if she had gone for the lesser post. As it turned out, she was correct in her prophecies although she was a bit before her time — about seven hundred years.

"She lived at the time of Dante Alighieri," Milton observed.

"Yes, she did, but her prophecies were meant for the millennium and that is why she has returned."

"Another imagined golden age or the breaking of the seal of apocalypse?" Milton asked.

"Time will tell," Madame Bauhaud said, reaching for her glass of wine and returning to the Aladdin text.

4.

In the dark before dawn, Sarge shook Candler awake. "I want to explain to you about the book again."

"Yes," Candler replied, rubbing his eyes, sitting up. "What is it?"

Sarge proceeded to talk to Candler for thirty minutes or so about the contents of the book, what it suggested, what meanings could be gleaned from it.

Tilting his head, listening closely, Candler finally said: "This is what you told me yesterday about the book — in exactly the same words. Why? Why are you repeating it?"

"What do you remember of yesterday?" Sarge said. "You remember only your own interpretations. You did not listen to what I said."

"I did...I did listen," countered Candler. "What are you doing, why are you doing this?"

"I am here to insult you," Sarge said, turning away.

5.

Both Milton and I happened to be in Quebec City at the same time several weeks later. The hope of a week's rest and recuperation had drawn me to a small hotel in the old town while Milton was there to help settle the estate of his uncle on the paternal side. We decided to meet at the revolving bar at the top of Hôtel Le Concorde just outside the walls of the old city. The bar was called l'Astral.

After taking the swift elevator up several dozen floors, I walked the inner circle of the bar and found Milton sitting at a table with a lit candle and a glass of Pernod. I sat. We exchanged pleasantries and I ordered the same.

"On the way up here I stopped for lunch along the highway at a St. Hubert B.B.Q." Milton made his opening gambit. "I remember sitting there eating my chicken and asking myself: St. Hubert...St. Hubert... was he a martyr slowly barbecued on a spit? I asked the waitress who regarded me, for the duration of my meal, as if I were completely mad."

"You are, Milton, no doubt about it."

We toasted each other. "Cheers."

"How's Candler coming?" Milton asked.

"It's driving me crazy, actually. I need a break from it for a few weeks. Something's happening with the time element in his story. I just can't follow it. You'd think with a simple linear journey like that I could keep it straight, one day following another following another, but it seems to keep shattering into fragments.

It's as if he takes two steps forward and one step back. Drawn to Lhasa and repelled at the same time, but in the end fated to arrive there. Anyway, I realize now that I have to go to England. Do more research. I'll leave in a month or so."

We drank.

"I never finished my story the other night...you fell asleep."

It didn't take much to encourage Milton to continue his tale of Madame Bauhaud and the strange Guglielma. Slowly the bar turned above the thousand pinprick lights of the city, it could have been any city seen from this height, and the great darkness filled in the background. I thought at one point of how it seemed we were sitting on a huge clock, barely noticing that we were turning, one moment to the next, going round and round.

Madame Bauhaud and Guglielma, Milton explained, were on the path to glory and wisdom through exegesis, or the critical study of books. Through wide reading and their exegesis of secret texts, they had concluded that Guglielma was a product of parthenogenesis. Last time around she had really been the Holy Spirit but had to pretend to be the one true Pope; this time she was the Virgin Mary. Suddenly Milton suspected that both women were quite mad and that they saw his role as the New Christ. This feeling grew and grew in him and eventually caused his exile from the place. In fact, he felt he had actually been "exiled" from the Villa Bauhaud; he didn't just leave. It was much more deep an involvement than that. Milton told the story of Guglielma's bizarre previous life and her intrigues with the Popess. How the net of plots began to close in on her and how she was eventually burned at the stake.

"They were bitterly disappointed when they found out I wasn't the New Christ. After three weeks of this, I was starting to go a bit bonkers myself — all the wine and the late nights and the study. It was wonderful for a while and they taught me some valuable lessons — but such crazies. I'm glad we parted as friends. She gave me an ancient Tibetan book as a present. I'll have to show it to you someday."

Almost invisibly, the bar revolved. The lights of the city and the stars in heaven, which seemed inches beyond the glass walls of the bar, flickered. "Two years later, I heard through my mother that the villa burned to the ground, both Madame Bauhaud and Guglielma died in the fire and, of course, all the books were lost."

CHAPTER X

1.

Word moved quickly down the column of soldiers
as they climbed the narrow mountain path. It sounded
like a hissing whisper as the word was repeated
again and again from one man to the next:
"lost...lost...lost." When word reached General
Macdonald, confined still to his *doolie* hefted by a
handful of Ghurkas, the news caused an explosion
of hysteria: "Lost, my God, we're lost...we'll all
die...we're lost in these god-forsaken mountains...lost!" Ottley and Colonel Younghusband were
riding back through the crowd of soldiers, looking
for Candler and Sarge. Their favoured Tibetan scout

knew little about this country. As soon as Ottley saw Macdonald and heard his shouts, he jumped down from his horse and slapped the sick man hard in the face until he was blubbering and weeping, and silenced. He knew it wouldn't do to have the men spooked by their own commanding officer. So he did what would have been forbidden in normal situations. Younghusband continued his search and soon found Candler and Sarge at the rear of the column.

"Candler, it seems we've taken a wrong turn somewhere. Perhaps your man knows this country? Do you?" Younghusband asked Sarge, turning to him sitting on his pony.

"I do."

"Would you please tell us then where we are going?"

"Nowhere," Sarge answered. "Going nowhere. This mountain . . . we have been circling this same mountain for two days."

"Why didn't you tell me?" Candler asked him crossly.

"I like this mountain," Sarge observed.

Just then, across a wild stream that racketed down a narrow gorge, three monks and an old woman appeared around a large boulder, walking downhill. They were holding wooden prayer wheels in their hands, spinning them and mumbling their chants. When they saw the confused and waiting column of soldiers they pointed, made some comments among themselves and laughed uproariously.

"You see," Sarge observed, "they are walking correctly. We have been going counter-clockwise. We must turn around and all will be set right."

The column turned, the men grumbled, Young-husband rode to his place at the front and the army was once again on its way to Lhasa.

2.

July 24, 1904   Khamba Partsi

No matter how it conjures future time, no matter how it divines the past, the book is always in present time which is to say no time at all: a cloud-mountain swollen with snow.

3.

As the long straggling expedition column descended the slopes of the mountains, they left behind an area peopled by nomadic shepherds and entered a region of small farms punctuated by tiny crumbling villages that were almost indistinguishable from the surrounding cliffs, except for the ever-present baying of dogs, the stooped vultures on nearby houses and the smiling friendly villagers themselves who came out to stare at the hundreds of foreigners dressed in outlandish costume parading past their hovels. Near one of these villages, the expedition made camp and prepared for a rest of several days.

Early in the evening, Sarge and Candler headed for the village. Sarge seemed to be trying to recall something.

"Where are we going?" Candler asked.

"*Chang*," said Sarge.

"*Chang*? What's *chang*?"

"I believe you English call it beer," Sarge grinned. "I have heard tales about a *chang*-maker in this village. He is renowned throughout the land. That is why I had Younghusband and Ottley camp here."

"What? What are you saying?" Candler asked.

Sarge ignored the question. "There's the house!" He pointed and broke into a trot. Candler followed.

After the briefest of introductions, during which the man acted as if he had house guests drop by from Britain every day, the two visitors entered the rough house with its greystone walls and dirt floor. Sarge and the *chang*-maker soon learned that they had a mutual friend and they spent some minutes discussing him. The *chang*-maker, sitting on a rug like the others, was thin as a barley stalk, with a wizened face mapped with deep wrinkles. His eyes shone like two pure lakes in the midst of that scored and weather-beaten land.

Disappearing into a back room, he soon returned with a large jug and three cups. Handing the cups around, he began to pour for Candler, saying simply,

"*Chang say...chang say.*" Candler asked Sarge what "*say*" meant and learned that it was the word for gold. He explained that the *chang*-maker was known for two kinds of *chang*: gold *chang* and *mutig*, or pearl, *chang*. *Chang say* was the best. "Not that *chang mutig* should ever be refused," Sarge was quick to add.

They drank. Candler found the taste intriguing. Pleasant and unpleasant at the same time. Sour and sweet. Sarge and the *chang*-maker drank quickly, talking and gesticulating. One or the other kept filling Candler's cup even if it wasn't empty. Candler stared at the cup. It was an odd shape. Rather shallow. It dawned on him, as it had once before, that he was drinking from a portion of skull, perhaps an animal skull but quite possibly human. Sarge looked at him. "*Ka gomgiy,*" he said. "Thirsty. Drink. You have been thirsty for years." He held the cup up to him and smiled warmly.

Something in Candler suddenly made him want to weep. Perhaps he was getting drunk. Yes, he was thirsty. He had been thirsty for as long as he could remember. Taking the cup from Sarge's hand, he drank deeply, with abandon, letting the liquid flow down his throat in large cooling draughts. Sarge and the *chang*-maker laughed happily when they saw this and drank more lustily themselves. The jug disappeared and returned full again. The *chang*-maker poured. They drank and now all three were laughing, at nothing, at their own drunkenness, at the crazy world.

The *chang*-maker leaned forward and whispered to Sarge.

"He wants to know…" Sarge turned to explain. Candler looked at him blankly, sighed…and passed out.

The next morning he awoke in his tent. Sunlight was beaming full in his face, for Sarge who sat close by watching him had pulled back the tent flap to let in the light and air. Candler felt curiously refreshed. The sunlight was not quite blinding. It shone with a painful brilliance. Candler became aware that he had a strange choice at that moment. If he resisted the brilliance of the light, it would hurt. If he gave in to it, it became something that passed through him, igniting him, burning off all the dark places inside, turning to ashes all his hesitations and fears and doubts about himself, his life, everything. "Good morning," Sarge nodded.

4.

Candler and Sarge dismounted near a small lake. They had left the expedition camp an hour before, riding north through a series of intricate valleys and defiles. Sarge had said little, only that he wished to show Candler a special place, an unusual lake with turquoise waters.

Sarge told the journalist to sit. "Make yourself comfortable," he said.

Candler sat in the grass and crossed his legs. The sun was warm and he could smell the fresh green grass in the air.

Sarge sat next to him. "It is good to breathe," he said.

Candler felt the clean empty air coming in and out of his lungs. He gazed at the lake. It was indeed a strange shade of turquoise and seemed to be rippling with the soft breeze.

"Watch." Sarge pointed to the surface of the lake. Quite relaxed, Candler paid attention to the water, the way it shifted and tossed. He readjusted his position and gazed at it again. Then he noticed something. Drifting to the surface of the water from the depths came words, cursive as seaweed and flickering like fish. He saw them beginning to glow at about ten feet below the surface as they rose. When they reached the air they dissolved as other words kept rising to take their place. He looked at Sarge who smiled and continued watching the water. Candler looked again. He watched for a long time and always the words kept rising to the surface and dissipating. After a long while, the two men stood and walked to the water's edge. Candler found it odd that the water refused to offer a reflection of their faces or of the surrounding mountains.

5.

Long before I had ever heard the word "Tibet," the idea of Tibet had revealed itself to Milton. For years he had been longing to visit the mountain kingdom, but over time due to various financial and political constraints, Tibet had always remained out of reach. Thus it was that Tibet took on a metaphorical quality for Milton. Going to Tibet had nothing to do with movement through space and, as he once explained, everything to do with movement through time. It also had a lot to do with barbecuing.

Milton wasn't quite sure when the idea of a barbecue had first entered his head. He recalled that it must have been early in his eighteenth summer, a few short years after the incident with the neighbour lady's underclothes, which still lingered over summer evenings in the backyard like the distant charred smell of a burnt-out ruin. Even though new neighbours had arrived in the autumn after the fateful fire, still the sight of clean white wash hanging on the clothesline was enough to darken Milton's sun-filled reveries. The backyard would never be quite the same.

The fifties was a time when barbecuing was taking hold of North American consciousness. Milton later believed it had some strange connection to the fear of nuclear holocaust and the need to come to know fire, the need to meet that fear head on, at least in some small way. There was also the need, he explained, to connect with something elemental at a time when life was becoming more and more of, what he called, a "technological cartoon." He had the same explanation for the widespread use of tobacco — it wasn't the taste people craved, it was the flame, the connection to something elemental, if only for a moment, in the flare of the match or lighter. At any rate, it was the mid-fifties and barbecue fit the bill.

In a corner of the backyard, Milton cleared a space, pulling out a dishevelled row of weeds that grew against the picket fence, and spaded up the turf. He measured. He drew plans. He consulted with his father who was all in favour of the project. A brick barbecue would certainly be a fine replacement for the old three-legged metal contraption that had started, late the previous summer, threatening to thrust its load of white-hot coals onto the tennis shoes of whoever was turning hamburgers.

If nothing else Milton was intellectually precocious. He decided he was not just building a barbecue — he was also involved in a Vedic ritual of constructing a fire altar to the two-faced fire god, Agni. He decided that lamb chops would be the appropriate first meal.

When Milton mixed concrete he knew he wasn't just mixing concrete — he was preparing the element earth. When he added water from the garden hose, it was the elemental waters of life that came pouring, hot with afternoon sunlight, from the mouth of that long green snake. The element, air, of course, was no problem, being plentiful enough to feed hundreds of such altars in the backyards of the entire neighbour-

171

hood. And, last but not least, fire, which was the entire purpose of this suburban re-enactment of creation.

Milton noticed the hot plastic smell from the hose as the water dribbled into the concrete powder. I am consecrating a sacred space, he whispered to himself, constructing a mandala at the centre of which stands a tabernacle of fire, a sanctum sanctorum of flame. Already he could smell the lamb chops, could hear them sizzling on the grate. He didn't even bother to ask himself how it was that his thoughts could move from the sublime to the sensual without a flicker of hesitation.

The sun beat down for the entire two weeks he spent in early July building the barbecue. By eleven in the morning he would start to sweat, soaking his white T-shirt while carrying bricks from a pile left by a delivery truck to the side of the driveway. Then he mixed cement by hand with an old hoe in a long metal bin. At noon, his mother would bring out lemonade and a plate of peanut butter and jelly sandwiches to join him for lunch at the picnic table, which sat in the sliver of shade thrown by the house. She would survey the rising construction with its two wings and open central ovens, and later, the solid chimney that would take the smoke into the open upstairs windows of neighbouring houses. Sometimes Milton would talk about his ideas, about Vedic ritual, and the god Agni, and the idea of a mandala. She would stare at him, fascinated, a bit frightened even, not comprehending a word. "You and your books, Milton!" she would say. "I hope it helps you get into law school, that's all I care about. If you don't go to law school, your Uncle Harry will never forgive us."

Uncle Harry was a downtown lawyer, Milton's father's oldest brother. He was considered one of the wealthiest lawyers in Montreal, lived in a vast stone house on the tony slopes of Mont Royal and had promised to help send Milton to law school.

Milton's mother had just taken a bite from her sandwich when Milton announced, "I think I'd rather go to Tibet than law school." She looked at him, dumbfounded, the lump of sandwich halfway down. There was no question about being able to swallow it now. A garbled "Hunh?" fought its way out of her throat. Why had he said it? He didn't know himself what had prompted that bizarre statement, only that the thought had been wavering in his subconscious for quite a long time and stating it felt right. In fact, it was a relief. "I've decided not to go to law school." He didn't bother to ask if Uncle Harry would want to finance his journey to Tibet instead.

6.

It seemed they always met in rooms without windows. Both of them were more comfortable in rooms without windows, rooms at the centre of vast dark palaces where their voices would be lost long before they ever reached the clear light of day. In fact, daylight never reached these rooms; they were bathed in perpetual darkness or were lit by lamps or long tapers that merely deepened the shadows in the corners and cast a light cold as marble.

The two monks always leaned together when they spoke, eyes fixed on the other's ear, the swirl descending. To an outsider it would appear that they were hearing each other's confession — and perhaps they were, perhaps they were.

"He has no intention of sending any troops to Lhasa...none...so tell your lama to run and hide wherever he can...or let him face the British if he wishes...I don't really care...it's none of my business."

Dorjieff nodded his round head slowly as Rasputin's words fell on his ears. "Besides," the Russian monk continued, "your lama has made it clear he doesn't want Russians in Tibet any more than he wants the British."

"This is true," Dorjieff sighed, "quite true."

A servant entered the room and bowed. "The Tsar will see you now," he announced.

7.

When Candler brought up the trip to the strange turquoise lake with words rising to the surface, hoping to discuss it, hoping to find some reason for such a phenomenon, Sarge denied having ever been there, denied having taken Candler to any such place, denied that such a lake existed. Later that afternoon, Candler rode out in an attempt to find the lake again. He couldn't. After five hours of searching, the sun was descending, spilling down a long valley that ended in a groove between two mountains. Candler stopped. He turned in the saddle looking back the way he had come. Turned again, surveying the valley, wondering. The horse wheezed, seeming exceedingly loud in the almost absolute silence.

On his return, Sarge was waiting outside their tent on a stool, taking in the last rays of the sun. "There really is no lake," he explained to Candler as the Englishman sat on the ground next to him. "I created that scene for you...no, I am wrong...you created that scene for yourself, I had nothing to do with it." Candler picked up some dirt and watched it sift through his fingers. An involuntary shudder passed through Candler as he gazed down at the ground. "Come. Let's walk," Sarge said, standing and helping Candler up.

After about fifteen minutes of walking, Candler gave himself up to the easy motion and the realization that there was no rational explanation. No meaning behind the lake, no meaning to Tibet, no meaning to this expedition. No meaning to his life, either, he supposed, and laughed to himself. He walked for a long time in silence. Sarge too was silent. The earth and the heavens were silent. The dark came on and it too was silent. The stars began to appear, also silent. The mountains were silent. For a moment, only a moment, Candler's heart too was silent.

CHAPTER XI

———— ✦ ————

1.

The expedition, a two-day march from Lhasa, had encamped beside a swollen, fast-moving river, the Tsangpo. Younghusband decided they would spend several days there, waiting for supplies and preparing for the final march into the city. He also secretly hoped that the Dalai Lama would end his silence and negotiate a truce, now that the British had shown they were serious about going as far as the capital itself if necessary. Since the passage of the Karo La, there had been a few small skirmishes but no determined resistance. He doubted, however, that they would be allowed into Lhasa without a fight.

The time would also be spent gathering a number of coracles, or skin-covered boats, from the local population, to be used for the crossing. These were also known as "carcass boats" and, indeed, the Tibetan version looked like an upside-down gutted animal, scooped out and dried. Candler did not look forward to negotiating the turbulent river in one of these unwieldy vessels. The coracles would be added to the four Berthon boats the troops had brought along with them.

As it turned out, two ferry boats were found downstream, barges really, with horses' heads at the prow. These old vessels were capable of holding up to a hundred men and saved the expedition several weeks of crossing time. Candler thought there was something almost Greek about crossing into the Lhasa region on the back of a great horse.

Late on the first evening after their arrival on the banks of the Tsangpo, Younghusband had Colonel Ottley summoned to his tent. Dark had fallen. As Young-husband discussed the plans, Ottley listened and sharpened his knife on a square of stone he held in his left hand, the conversation punctuated with sandy strokes of the knife.

"Have you looked into our problem?" Young-husband began.

"Yes, I met with the scouts and we travelled to several villages where they trust the people. It is not quite clear, but it appears that Candler's manservant has been keeping the enemy informed about our movements. He sneaks off in the middle of the night and probably meets a rider in the hills who reports back to their camp. I believe that somewhere between here and Lhasa, they will attack in full force."

"Has anyone actually seen him do this?"

"My scouts know these people as well as the land. I trust them beyond questioning. I trained them myself."

"Fine. But do not make a move until we know for sure," Younghusband cautioned.

"I believe we know enough."

"No, we do not know enough and that is all I am going to say about it. Do you understand, Mr. Ottley?"

A rising doubt had entered Younghusband's mind. Ottley was quite capable of riding off on his own, and had been a little too quick to accept full command of the troops during Macdonald's illness. More than a bit too sure of himself. Too cocky. Arrogant. Nevertheless Younghusband felt he would carry a thing through, he wouldn't back down from a fight.

"How was Macdonald today?"

Ottley shook his head as he swirled the long, bone-handled knife across the sharpening stone. "Worse. I fear he won't make it."

"What shall we do with him? Send him back?"

"It's very strange. He goes back, he gets better. He heads towards Lhasa, he grows worse. I don't understand it. He does wish to finish the journey, though. He wants to go on."

"Then that is what he will do — on to his fate," Younghusband concluded.

"And to ours," Ottley said, dragging his thumb across the blade of the knife.

2.

"Italians love to talk, so the old lady in the store where I bought the olive oil couldn't help but give me her family recipe for spaghetti sauce five minutes after I met her, even though the recipe had been handed down in secret from generation to generation, whispered from 'momma' to 'figlia,' in numerous villages up and down the slopes of Sicily. Divulging the recipe to a wider audience would have been considered a *peccato mortale* in the old country and punishable in the same way that divulging the secrets of the Cosa Nostra was punishable; but this was North America where everything was new, even the old kitchen secrets. I guess she thought I had an honest face." I leaned over the white porcelain stove, holding the handle of a black cast-iron frying pan in my left hand, pouring olive oil from a squarish glass bottle with my right hand, turning now and then to direct my conversation to Milton who was sitting at the kitchen table set for two.

The olive oil, gold and thick, slid across the bottom of the pan. I then peeled several large waxy garlic cloves and squeezed them through the press into the hot oil where they sizzled contentedly. Milton left the kitchen and went to retrieve something from the living room. Meanwhile, with the side of a long knife I slid chopped onions, celery and green pepper off a scarred wooden cutting board into the pan. More sizzling. The animated odour of garlic filled the air of the kitchen.

Milton returned with a bottle of wine and began removing the cork. "Chianti Classico '81," he said. "I hope there's no ox-blood in it."

Nodding, I cut up half a dozen fresh, ripe plum tomatoes and tossed them into the pan, then added seven medium-sized bay leaves, whole. Putting a lid on what was quickly becoming a vegetable slush, I opened a can of tomatoes and a small can of tomato paste. Lifting the lid, I sloshed the tomatoes into the frying pan and began cutting the whole tomatoes into smaller pieces. Then I took nine large black olives, of the sort one buys bulk, not the tasteless canned variety and, with a small paring knife, sliced them away from their hard pits. This pile was added to the mélange.

Milton busied himself shining the two wineglasses, holding each up to the overhead kitchen light to determine that they were, in fact, absolutely without blemish. The wine breathed. "I absolutely must tell you about the pilgrimage Madame Bauhaud and Guglielma took to see the Blessed Virgin Mary at...now where was it...have you an atlas?"

"In the office, with the dictionaries on the desk," I replied without looking up from the bags and bottles of herbs and spices I was arranging. Let's see now, how does that go, the order is all-important. Rosemary not quite generously, basil generously, thyme slightly, oregano most generously, a few long shakes of mild curry powder and the secret ingredient in just the right amount. I placed them in a line.

Milton returned with the atlas. "*Dent's Canadian School Atlas*," he announced. "A classic."

I then spooned the tomato paste out of the can into the sauce, and mixed it. Filling the empty can with tap water, I poured three-quarters of it into the pan and set the remainder on the stove between the burners. Mixing the whole with a flat wooden spatula, I forced the water and the paste and the cooked vegetables together. Milton consulted the atlas.

As I removed two jars from the fridge, Milton looked up. "What's that — the secret ingredient?"

"Not really," I replied without stopping my work, "just several elements the addition of which I have learned add favourably to the overall sapidity." I stirred in a large spoonful of honey, a small spoonful of molasses and several glugs of Tamari soy sauce. I then added about two fingers of red wine from a half-filled bottle. "In fact, the secret ingredient is soon to come. You will see. Cooking is like alchemy, Milton, my friend, it is not only a matter of ingredients but also a matter of timing and the order in which things are added and the state of mind of the cook. A great spaghetti sauce is like a work of fiction. Oh, the noodles...!"

Grabbing a pot, I filled it with water and placed it on a burner. Then it was time for the herbs and spices. Milton had returned to the atlas, ogling the long Italian leg. "Must have been quite the lady that posed for this," he said. I was busily stirring the thickening sauce that would spout little red geysers, Italian Vesuvios, if it was not attended to every few moments.

The scent of rosemary wafted from my palms as I rubbed the tiny dried sticks together. I tossed them in. Always mix in the spice or herb before adding the next one. Where did I learn that? Spaghetti Rule Number 402: the logic of mixing herbs into sauces. Next, a fistful of basil. Can't resist smelling it, each one, as they go in. Mix. A minor flurry of thyme. Mix. Cover the whole with a dried bed of oregano. Smell it. Mix. Some say one should never taste the sauce until it is finished — a rule I have never been able to support. A half-teaspoonful, to ensure that all elements are moving in a beneficent direction. Mmmm. Delish. Several marigold rows of mild curry. A red tiger with yellow stripes. Mix. It's a wonder the numberless ghost-mommas of Palermo don't rise from their graves and tear me limb from limb — curry, curry!? *Vietato! Vietato!* I can hear the aproned hordes screaming. Whoreson! Bastard son of an immigrant fast-food cook! Ah well, what can I do? I plead poetic licence. And now for the coup de grâce... careful...careful...not too much...

Milton looked up. "What are you doing? You're hovering over that sauce as if it were about to turn into a pan of molten gold."

"It has, it has!" I enthused. "The secret ingredient." I took a deep whiff from the small bottle lost in my fist. "You know they execute you if you try to smuggle this stuff out of Madagascar. Cloves. That's what the old witch in the olive oil store told me to use. 'Cloves,' she said, with her almost toothless mouth, leaning close so the other customers couldn't hear. 'Cloves,' she breathed in my ear and cloves she was right. Cloves — the little nails that hold it all together."

"When will you stop gushing over it so we can eat?" Milton asked.

"Anyway, I think it was near Pisa where they went to see the BVM," Milton said a few minutes later when we were seated and eating.

"Hmm...there's something missing." I gazed at a coiled rope of spaghetti on my fork, dark red with sauce. Suddenly it dawned on me. "Aw no, I forgot the ground beef! I'm not a vegetarian!"

"It's all right. Tastes delicious," Milton said soothingly. "In fact, it's fantastic."

"You're right; it's quite good," I commented. "So go ahead. What happened?"

"Well, it was in the swampy area around Pisa, in a small rock outcropping near a little-travelled dirt road. A typical story, really. Twelve-year-old girl has vision of BVM, local faithful flock to the sight in hopes of curing asthma, healing broken limbs, multiplying investments, et cetera. The usual carnival arises — vendors selling bottled lemonade and bitters, holy cards and plastic-framed paintings of Jesus, the kind with eyes that follow you wherever you roam. Madame Bauhaud had heard the inevitable rumours about miracle cures. At that time, she and Guglielma had been reading quite deeply into Tibetan beliefs in local deities and other such beings. She had also read that the Tibetans believed that dreams dreamt at dawn were true dreams. This was also believed by Medieval Italians, and can be found in Dante. As it turned out, Madame Bauhaud dreamt early one morning that she and Guglielma should check out the little girl, Violetta, near Pisa. So they did. As they arrived at the shrine, the little girl was having a vision. The crowd was oohing and aahing as the girl swayed back and forth and prayed. Madame Bauhaud couldn't see the BVM but Guglielma could. As soon as the BVM turned to Guglielma and met her eyes, the smoky Virgin melted into a snake that crawled off and into a nearby hole in the ground. No one else in the crowd, except Madame Bauhaud, noticed the snake — they were all watching Violetta. When Madame Bauhaud saw the snake, she leaned over to Guglielma and whispered 'naga' and pointed. Guglielma explained what had happened. The little girl then came out of her trance, the crowd dispersed and no one ever returned to that place again, at least not for visionary experiences. But the really odd thing was — the locals say that at the moment of the girl's withdrawal from trance, at the moment when the Virgin dissolved and the snake entered the hole, every adult male in the region felt a sharp pain in the testes. What do you think of that?"

"*Nagas?* Candler spoke of *nagas*, snake-beings in Tibetan lore, also known to hand on sacred or secret books. Hmmm," I mused, twirling spaghetti onto my fork. "The sauce thickens."

3.

Sitting in his tent, Candler again weighed the package in his hand. Yes, of course, a figure, a Buddha or another of their gods. One can tell it is a figure by the way the string wraps around the shoulders, defining the head, nothing more than a stone statue, that's all, just a figure in stone, nothing special, a piece of carved rock, a man in robes, a calm face, a seated figure, quiet, peaceful — then why does it feel as if it might explode in my hands? And the weight, it's uncanny, unnaturally heavy for the size, it seems like some kind of bound power, a force wrapped and held tight, thus increasing its urge to expand. He bowed forward and replaced it in his trunk, with care.

Late that night, Candler woke from a deep sleep. He could hear Sarge's low snore but there was something else. He listened. Heard his own heart pounding. Leaning out of his cot, he saw a boot catching a wedge of moonlight that found its way through the tent's open flaps. Open flaps? I thought I closed them. As his eyes adjusted to the dark, he realized there was a leg attached to the boot! Without thinking he reached down, grabbed the lower leg and pulled as hard as he could, sending the body flying. In an instant, Sarge and he were up grappling with the shadow. They fell into the wall of the tent, which collapsed on top of them. The shouts and struggling had awakened men in other tents who came running. Someone brought a lit lamp. Sarge and Candler crawled out from under the canvas. The third figure remained still. Candler knew who it was without looking. Throwing off the tent, he revealed the face of Ottley, eyes and mouth agape, his body twisted around so that it rested on his own hands. Flipping him over, Candler saw in Ottley's fist the bone handle of a knife. The blade was thrust up to the hilt in Ottley's belly. Candler was glad Major O'Connor said it first: "He must have fallen on his own knife. Poor devil."

"I knew he would never cross the river into the region around Lhasa," Sarge explained later. "The fool. I was beginning to like him. An arrogant, difficult man but there was something about him. Disciplined. No laziness. He was in the habit of sharpening his knives at night — a bad practice. The people around here, they say it is a bad omen."

Candler was beginning to regret ever having come on the expedition. For the first time in many months he experienced an intense longing for England, for his wife, for some kind of normal life.

It was as if Sarge could read his mind. "Your life will never be normal again, Englishman. You will go home but all will have changed because you will have changed. Nothing stays the same, ever."

Candler looked at him, not even surprised that his mind could be read. Yes, he had changed, everything had changed. He nodded. "I want to go home," he stated simply, like a child.

Sarge shook his head. "No. You can't. You have no home."

4.

The next day they buried Ottley with the appropriate military honours. Afterward, for the first time in a long while, Candler sent his report by telegraph to the *Daily Mail*. Actually, he wrote it out and handed it to a rider who was returning down the supply line. It would be sent from the nearest point on the telegraph line sixty miles away. The rider had brought with him a bag of mail, weeks old now, but pounced on by the men as if it were gold. Candler received a letter from Veronica, his wife.

He was surprised how adamant she was about it, although, strangely enough, he no longer needed convincing. She explained that she would never leave

England. She had no desire to live in India. She asked him to come home at the earliest opportunity so they could get on with their lives. He was not surprised at this. In fact, he had never been able to imagine Veronica mixing with the other wives at Simla. It was impossible. She was too honest to play the games it was necessary to play in order to get along in a constricted colonial society. For his part, it took him quite a long while to realize that he too had no desire to settle in India. But now something had been set in motion. He would begin his return home on reaching Lhasa and finishing his assignment.

Veronica had also included in the letter a clipping from the *Daily Mail*. It read:

AGAINST TIBET CAMPAIGN

A curious blending of Englishmen and Orientals denounced the Tibet Expedition at the Westminster Palace Hotel yesterday afternoon, the New Reform Club, the Indian National Congress and the London Indian Society having joined forces for the purpose of raising a protest against what was described as "an act of constitutional illegality" and a scheme which was foredoomed to failure.

Bearded Hindus of every caste and every shade were there, "Lord Salisbury's black man," Mr. Dadabhai Naoroji, being among them.

The objections of the demonstrators seemed to be principally based on the assertion that the

Tibetans are a mild, peaceable race, who have broken no treaties and done nothing to deserve the sending of an expedition into their country.

A resolution was passed "protesting against the armed invasion of Tibet, which will be a heavy burden upon the already over-taxed natives of India."

When Candler showed the clipping to Young-husband, he did not expect a comment. Younghusband read it, handed it back to Candler, looked sadly at the distant mountains and said, "I fully agree. And you, Mr. Candler, what is your feeling?"

"I too agree. We do not belong here. There is no reason for it."

"Perhaps there is a reason, somewhere, Mr. Candler. But I sincerely hope that we may finish our journey to Lhasa, make our entreaties there and then leave this country to its own devices, as it so ardently wishes. It will be as if none of it ever happened."

As they stood outside the tents, the river rushing nearby, Candler remembered something Sarge had told him. "No, sir, I disagree. We do not know yet exactly how this journey will affect us but I believe it will not be forgotten. In fact, I believe it will affect us in ways we cannot even imagine."

"You may be right, Mr. Candler, you may be right."

5.

Milton and I were out for a walk along Rue Sherbrooke on a Saturday afternoon. Mont Royal leaned nearby like a protective mother overseeing our safety. The slightest hint of spring was in the air.

"When are you leaving for England?" Milton asked.

"Soon, I've finally finished a number of small projects I had to get out of the way," I said. "I want to see my Auntie Liz, whom I'm sure I've mentioned to you before. You know, I saw a photograph of her recently and I was struck by an uncanny resemblance she had to Candler's Tibetan servant, a fellow named Sarge. It was quite strange. I'd very much like to talk to her."

"I'll bet."

"What have you been up to?"

Milton's eyes sparkled. "I've been studying a few Tibetan texts... and putting them into practice. The thing I like about the Tibetan myths is that they come with practical means of application for the attainment of transcendence, unlike a lot of other myths which, for us today, are just stories, albeit archetypal stories but mere stories nonetheless.

"Also, look at this..." He held his wristwatch up for me to see. At first I didn't notice anything, and then I saw words scratched on the hour and minute hands. "Buddhas" scratched on the one and "Wake!" scratched on the other. "Like Tibetan prayer flags and prayer wheels. I like the idea that clocks and watches and various other timepieces can be put to service on our behalf, exhorting us in their innocence. You see, time is the key..."

But then an ambulance roared past, followed closely by a long red firetruck, sirens wailing. I saw Milton's mouth moving but heard nothing. Something made me refrain from asking Milton to repeat himself. Perhaps it was the way he looked when he had finished — as if the topic had been concluded in perfect precision. He looked pleased with himself.

I changed the subject. "By the way, I found out something interesting recently. Candler stopped off in Italy on his way back from India. I'm not sure why and I'm not sure what he did there or where he went but the idea intrigues me."

It was then that Milton finally noticed my left arm. I had it in a sling but it had been covered by my overcoat which I unbuttoned when the sun had warmed the air sufficiently. "What happened?"

"Nothing," I said. "I just want to find out what it's like to function with only one hand. A little experiment."

6.

Sarge shook Candler awake. "Come with me," he whispered, "and be quiet."

The first rays of dawn were thrusting up into the sky as the two men walked away from the tents. At some distance, behind a knoll, two horses were tethered. Mounting and managing to avoid the guards, they rode off.

Up a narrow path between two rocky cliffs. Loose stones all around. Glancing up, Candler caught sight of a half-dozen vultures lined up along a cliff edge. One dropped off and swept down in a wide-ranging arc, disappearing from view. Soon the narrow path opened into a stone-strewn plateau. At the far end of the plateau under another cliff stood a huge flat rock and on this rock stood two men, Tibetans, hard at work with long knives. They appeared to be butchering something. Three vultures stood on the ground boldly snapping out for pieces of the prize.

Sarge pulled up at a discreet distance. They watched for a few moments as the men continued throwing pieces of raw meat to the vultures. Then one of the men poured what appeared to be flour into a large stone bowl. Taking a kind of hammer, he began to pound at one of the bones, smashing it into smaller and smaller bits.

"What are they doing?" Candler asked.

Sarge looked at him without smiling. "Sky burial. In Tibet this is what we do with the dead. A feast for the vultures."

Candler flinched. "Who is it — some old man from the village?"

Sarge laughed, then turned to Candler: "Ottley."

"My God!" Candler blurted out. "But he was buried! I saw it myself!"

"We dug him up," Sarge said simply. "Don't worry, he is better off this way. Believe me."

Sunlight glinted off one of the knives wielded by the men. "It is getting late. We must return," Sarge said.

CHAPTER XII

<hr />

1.

I picked up the phone after the second ring.

"Alex, is that you?" Milton barked. "How about I drive you to the airport next week? You're leaving on Tuesday, aren't you? Right. We'll go early, have a few drinks. I like the bar there. You know, the one with the kites."

"Sure, Milton, that'd be great."

"By the way, here's a travel quote you might like: 'Travel and travellers are two things I loathe — and yet here I am, all set to tell the story of my expeditions'...that's Claude Lévi-Strauss, first line of *Tristes Tropiques*. I'm astounded by the irony in that line. Irony, Alex, is the primary characteristic of our age. Negate, negate, negate. Then act anyway."

"Is it humbling?" I wondered. "What is it about irony that has captured the modern imagination?" Already the discussion was under a full head of steam heading out of port, ready for the long pull. I loathe long conversations, but here goes anyway.

"Humbling? Possibly." Milton was silent for a moment. "Duchamp. Duchamp's silence for twenty-five years — yet working in secret. That's the same irony, isn't it?"

"I take it back. It's not humility at all. It's ultimate confidence. No need for response from the outside world."

"Now that's humility," Milton exclaimed. "Hey, how's Tibet?"

"Snowy," I said. "I can't wait to get to England. I suspect Candler's private journal is in the British Library, crammed between the Magna Carta, Shakespeare's First Folio and the Gutenberg Bible. I want to see it. It might help clear up some questions I have."

"Wait a minute." Milton ran off, letting the phone dangle. I could hear it knocking rhythmically against the kitchen counter in his apartment as sounds echoed in the background: a refrigerator slamming, utensils rattling, a plate on the table. Milton returned. "Cheesecake," he mumbled. "My tapeworm loves it."

"Sounds good."

"So, tell me about Tibet. How's Candler? You scribbling or what?"

"I'd like to go. Asked the Red Chinese to send me for free — as part of a cultural exchange. They didn't answer my letter. No one answers my letters."

"Why bother going?" Milton said. "Nothing there. It's all in your head."

"I need inspiration. You know, Potala Palace, butter lamps in vast shadowy halls, monasteries housing ten thousand monks, yak brains, et cetera, et cetera."

"Yeah, I know," Milton commiserated. "But it's probably for the best that the Chinese didn't answer you. One peek at your notes and they'd have you strung up so fast your head would spin. They know you'll tell the world that the Chinese are committing genocide there. At the rate they're going, there won't be a Tibet in twenty years — or a Tibetan. Tibetans will be the new Jews, dispersed across the earth. Anyway, tell me more about snow country. What do you know?"

"Never been," I said.

"Imagine it," he replied. "Make it up. It's your life. Just don't exaggerate — that's lying."

"The exaggeration of nothing," I tried to explain, "is still big nothing."

"That's good, that's good, a great place to begin. Gotta run. Good to hear from you. Bye."

He hung up.

2.

August 10, 1904   Lhasa

Now that I am here in Lhasa, it is as if I am nowhere. A storm has passed. I feel a calmness in my heart, as well as a sad emptiness. But within that emptiness a light is shining — the light of the sun rising to the East. This morning Sarge and I watched it, the sun, surging up in a cleft between two mountains. We watched for I don't know how long — time means nothing to me now — and I realized I had been just watching the sun rise, nothing else. No turmoil of thoughts disturbing me. And now, to write it down, I feel as if something has been lost. Sarge has told me to throw this journal away, to be rid of it, that it is a burden for me. When the moment is right, I will pass it along, to someone...who?...I don't know. But for now, I will write in it no more.

3.

Candler then wrote a dispatch to the *London Daily Mail*, his first in weeks, and sent it off with the morning rider:

Lhasa must be the most hidden city in the world, caught as it is in a cup between nearby mountains and a sand embankment closing the valley. We couldn't see it until we were almost upon it, crossing a marsh alive with butterflies and dragon-flies flitting among the rushes and clematis. Nearby, cows grazed in rich fields while redshanks cried and a flock of teal pumped by. Within the town, numerous monks could be seen going about their business. Pilgrims who had come from other parts of the kingdom were discussing prices with shopkeepers under birds in wicker cages. While the residents looked at us as if an invading army arrived every day, the children pointed, ran about and shouted.

While the countryside was pleasant enough, the city itself was terribly dirty and there was a horrible stench in the air. Among all the filth and the ragged urchins you never knew when you might see pass by a proud Shapé dressed in gorgeous yellow silks and brocades, looking very much out of place and exotic in the drab setting.

Down a dank alley I noticed a bicycle without tyres and a sausage-making machine made in Birmingham, signs of the outside world, and I wondered how these strange objects found their way here before us, especially in light of the fact that the last Englishman to have visited this lost capital was Thomas Manning a hundred years ago. This land presents endless mysteries although I was sure this one had a logical explanation.

Colonel Younghusband has lectured the natives on the sanctity of British subjects after forcing the release of two men from Sikkim who had been imprisoned in a dark underground cell in the dungeon of the Potala Palace, the vast residence of the Dalai Lama who has fled we know not where. As the colonel lectured, I noted that the residents of the town who had been gathered looked at him as if he were not quite human, and even with the translation, I believe, did not comprehend a word.

Yesterday the troops held a gymkhana in a field located within the city. The games concluded with a horse race to which the head abbots of the local monasteries were invited. Excited as children, they soon learned how to place their bets on the totalizator.

The field itself was the most striking example I have ever seen of a natural amphitheatre with gently sloping hills providing comfortable seating for spectators and a perfectly flat circular space at the centre. It seemed as if we were sitting inside one of Mr. Wren's domes that had been up-ended, and I noted that this shape echoed the larger layout of the city itself. Then the horses ran and all else disappeared from my mind but the fate of my own bet.

4.

My Dear Dear Wife,

At last we have arrived in Lhasa. The final phase of the journey was easier than expected. A last major attack, predicted by our scouts, never materialized.

The Dalai Lama has fled, with the reviled Dorjieff. We believe they have gone to Russia, but no one is sure.

This city gives one the strangest feeling. Of course, there was no gold awaiting the soldiers. No Russians either. And very little of value to trade. Younghusband says we have made a disastrous mistake and places the blame squarely on Curzon's shoulders. Of course, he only speaks this way in private. The one structure of significance here is the Potala Palace which was the Dalai Lama's residence. Its size is beyond belief, especially considering the primitive building methods used in its construction. The many pilgrims who come here from other parts of Tibet can constantly be seen circumambulating the palace, making prostrations and fingering their beads. Their sweat mixes with the dust and some of them have bleeding foreheads from the practice. Our men mock them and call them primitive fools but I hold a certain admiration for their resolve and the depth of their beliefs. Otherwise the city is a paltry affair, nothing like a crown for the top of the world. It has an empty feel — this whole country does, but I feel it more here than elsewhere. And yet, my servant, Sarge, has come alive. He spends his time visiting old friends (he has many) and distant relatives, talking and drinking their version of ale. Often I accompany him, as there is little to do here while Younghusband awaits word from India about what we are to do next.

I am sure we will go back the way we came, leaving this land once again to its odd ways. That is the way these Tibetans would have it. To an Englishman, it seems like arrogance, the worst kind of stupidity and pride. My relationship with Sarge, however, is making me see another view. Perhaps things are not quite what they seem. Perhaps I am no longer a real Englishman.

Just before receiving your last letter (terribly delayed), I made the decision to return to England when my assignment here is finished. How wonderful to read that you were thinking along the same lines! I will request assignment somewhere in Britain (not with those crazy Scots, I hope!). I believe my travels are done. There are some things that I have to look into, sit down and look deeply into, some questions that have been raised. I do not mean to be mysterious. We will talk when I return.

Love,
Your Edmund

5.

Without warning, Candler awoke in the depths of the night in his tent on the outskirts of Lhasa, woke with a startling clarity of mind, and smelled the sea. He slipped out of the tent, leaving Sarge to his quiet sleep, and looked at the sky studded with myriad stars.

Nearby was Chakpori, the Iron Hill and the west gate to the city, and beyond, the imposing Potala Palace, dark and looming. He noted a pile of *mani* stones with Tibetan inscriptions on them at the foot of the gate. Again, he smelled a tinge of salt in the air, was overcome by its presence here at the top of the world, its profound suggestiveness, its softness seeming uncanny amid the mountains brilliant and hard in the moonlit dark. He felt the sea moving in his blood, its refreshing, relentless thrust and release, thrust and release, felt as well its larger tidal motion surging at a deeper level, a level almost beyond meaning. He drank the smell into his lungs, into his head, into his bones, glad to drown in it.

Leaning back from the page I was studying in the reading room, I looked up at the library's great dome, a strange thought circling in my head. These books around me are themselves mountains, replete with hidden valleys and meadows, full of lost civilizations, unclimbable peaks, ice caves, lonely villages inhabited by people with peculiar ways. The light that came in at the window was suddenly shot through with a rigid clarity, unlike the usual dirty, washed-out light of a London afternoon. It's the light of the mountains, I thought, a sliver, a shard of light escaped from the mountains, finding its way here by accident. I looked into that diamond light and found it was the light of all those pages gone blank, as if they were as they had once been...before words.

At that moment, I realized that I would never find Milton's book although I had the impression that it was not lost in the normal sense. In a quiet, internal kind of way it had shattered, exploded (a package of gun-cotton, a bomb after all!), disappearing and reappearing in all directions, in all times. Who knows where it would resurface, what future thoughts it might influence, what memories of the past it might reinterpret? I concluded that Milton's book was a bomb of ideas, a prolific bomb scattering its seeds in our dreams, in our visions, our memories. If we were barren, nothing would happen. If we offered fertile ground, however, anything was possible.

6.

After a month in Lhasa, Candler realized that they were just waiting, coming to terms with the fact that the entire exhibition was folly, had accomplished nothing. Oh, a treaty would eventually be signed but it meant nothing. They would demand terms from the Tibetans, an indemnity, a settlement, an agreement to respect British representatives in the future and an agreement not to allow any foreign power undue influence. But what would be changed? Candler had no answer. All the important men, the British and the Tibetans, would stand in a circle around a table on which rested the treaty, a great scroll, the ink not dry and yet already fading.

Meanwhile, an excruciating boredom set in, even more boring than the previous months, for now they had no goal, no hope, no mystery to strive towards. Perhaps this is what modern wars will be, Candler thought, done without reason, for no attainable end, and concluded due to a lack of energy.

Candler lay in the grass and gazed at the sky: It was empty, this war, this place, empty, haunted mountains adrift with birds of death. Terrifyingly empty, he said softly to himself, as he shaded his eyes from the noonday sun with his one good hand. Terrifying, and yet exhilarating at the same time...the colours here at dusk, uncannily brilliant yet meaning nothing, colours for which I lack names, and the people, animated as children one moment, trying to communicate with the foreign devils, but they turn around and it is as if you never existed, as if you never came...we will have no effect on this place; and yet I feel a profound change from having come here, and I see it in the others too, something indefinable and deep, something we once had, coming back after something else was stripped away, we will never shake this place, a kind of malaria that one might forget or escape for a while but it always recurs, a signal in the blood. And then it struck Candler with unpredictable force, that is, the power of truth: Yes, we have been conquered...drawn in, swallowed...and we will be spat out...and they will go on as if we were merely an odd-smelling wind...they will be untouched.

7.

Three months later, Candler was on a ship heading home from Bombay. The *Daily Mail* had asked him to disembark at Genoa for a month to cover a story there having to do with recent experiments by the Italian inventor, Guglielmo Marconi. The regular correspondent in Italy had died in a frightful accident, having been crushed by a wine barrel that rolled off a cart pulled by a bolting horse in Verona.

Sitting in his cabin, sipping tea, Candler thought about his last days with Sarge. He felt that Sarge was trying to tell him something, but he couldn't quite grasp it. As they took long meandering walks about the city and in the nearby hills, Sarge kept hinting that there was something for Candler to understand, but Candler couldn't put his finger on it. Perhaps it was meant to be that way.

The evening before the troops were to withdraw from Lhasa, the treaty having been signed in the depths of the Potala, Sarge took the correspondent to a small temple in an empty part of the city. There was nothing special about the temple — it was certainly unimpressive compared to the majesty of Potala Palace. While it contained the usual statues, paintings and butter lamps that one found in all the temples, these were not of a particularly rich or distinguished character.

But there was something about the temple that was different. It felt timeless, as if it had been there forever, would remain there forever. After pushing through the curtain of yak hair, Sarge sat down on a cushion and motioned Candler to do the same. The flames from the butter lamps pulsed like heartbeats. The statues of the Buddhas neither smiled nor frowned. A few monks in the half-lit room mumbled their incantations to themselves. The air was choked with clouds of sweet-smelling incense. Sarge merely sat and looked as if he was not about to say anything, so Candler also sat. Then Candler noticed that, for the first time since he had met Sarge, he stopped trying to figure him out. He stopped trying to understand what it was Sarge had been hinting at. The thought that had been nagging at him for months, in some sense, for his entire life, had stopped. Then Sarge touched his arm and turned towards the rear of the temple. Candler looked. They had just arrived, he thought, and here it was, morning already.

8.

My time in the reading room was drawing to an end. I knew I would have to return soon to Montreal and put my thoughts and notes in order and begin. The questions that had been plaguing me about Candler would never be answered, not in the way I expected. But it didn't matter. I had to move ahead, to go on despite my questions. Leaning forward from my seat at B4, I gazed down.

A tale. It's nothing more than a tale I look at on the page of the book in front of me. The spinning of someone's mind. But it comes out of a charged, shining emptiness. I note that the spaces between the words, between lines, are white, glowing — that was where the tale formed and came forward, surfacing. Several seats away, a man turns the pages of a book. When he finishes, he starts over again. It seems a great wind arises from this action, a wind that sweeps up in spirals through the dome. Within me too something surges. Looking around, I see a few clerks distributing books from carts, a few readers consulting the catalogue, but within the seeming quietude of the reading room I feel a frenzy of activity, the energy of all these words, all these minds spinning. The tens of thousands of volumes within my sight begin to vibrate and, as they do, the very walls of the room and the great dome itself slowly commence to spin. A prayer wheel, I'm inside a prayer wheel! Scraping back my wooden chair, I stand and look about. No one else seems to notice. A hallucination then? No, not a hallucination, but another tale, another tale rising. A distinct hum fills the air. I listen — it is all the words in all the books mingling into a single tone. Listening, enthralled, I glance up to the windows at the high base of the dome. They resonate with a painful clear light and then I see the column, the expedition marching there, Sarge in front followed by Younghusband and Ottley on their horses, then the other British officers and soldiers, Gurkhas, pack animals, coolies, sappers and gunners, cannons rolling, finally Candler at the end on his horse. Trying to keep my balance, clutching at the back of my chair, I turn watching them circle. Sarge urges his horse, not a pony now but a great silver beast with gold fittings, into a gallop — the rest of the column moves behind him. As the circle closes, Sarge's horse, approaching the rear of the column, takes the tail of Candler's horse in its mouth.

CHAPTER XIII

1.

In the airport, a woman friend I had not seen in several years stopped to chat. We talked for a few minutes about this and that, where we had been, where we were going.

"Too bad about Milton Kasma. You were a close friend of his, weren't you?"

"What do you mean? What's happened?"

"You didn't know? Of course, I'm sorry, you've been gone. Milton died about three weeks ago."

I leaned back against a wall, staring at the woman, listening as if from a great distance.

"It's not clear what happened. Somebody said he took poison, but then somebody else told me it was an accident. The police were called in — they even talked to me and I hardly knew him." She tilted her head. "I'm sorry, Alex."

The next several weeks I spent trying to find out what had happened, but no one had a clear answer. I was left with a great unanswerable ambiguity. No one could decide if it was suicide, an accident or foul play. I racked my brains trying to figure out who would want to kill Milton and came up empty-handed. A few former girlfriends, maybe, but no, not really. And an accident by poisoning seemed unlikely, although the police did mention that they found a variety of strange powders and leaves in his apartment. I didn't bother explaining to them that Milton was beginning his long-awaited research into medieval alchemy and that he had been collecting odd substances for years. I knew the police would not understand. Besides, Milton was extremely careful and painstaking in everything he did. An accident? No, Milton was not prone to accidents.

That left suicide as the only probable explanation. But that explanation raised all sorts of other unanswerable questions. Milton was never depressed, never suicidal, in the normal sense. Did that mean his was one of those rare suicides that is entirely justified and timely? Or did he flip? Or did he think he was justified and was wrong?

For weeks these questions plagued me. Everywhere I went I came upon places where we had talked. I searched our conversations, as well as I could remember them, for some kind of clue that would explain things. I sat on the slopes of Mont Royal, in the chill autumn air, and wondered why. I got angry, cursed Milton, wondered if I was wrong for cursing him, wondered what I could have done to change things. The clue never arrived.

Late one afternoon, sitting in the deli on Sherbrooke Street, I leaned over a half-cup of tepid coffee. My elbows were on the table. Once again I was thinking of Milton, how we had shared so many pastrami sandwiches and frenetic conversations over these same plastic table-tops. I was thinking of how death leaves all these ambiguities in its wake, questions that could not be answered. I was thinking of how wonderfully ambiguous Milton had been in life and why should his death be any different. I could feel my chest rising and falling with great sighs. Outside, beyond the large jars of pickles stacked right to the ceiling in the window, the first snow was falling, pure and white and delicious. I watched it drifting down, huge intricate flakes floating over the world, landing on sidewalks and streets and the shoulders of passersby, only to melt away.

2.

Candler had been back in London for a week. Sitting in the front room of the little house, he gazed into the fire that throbbed in the grate. Veronica had gone to bed, tired out by Edmund's mesmerizing tales. He had told her about Ottley and Younghusband, about Macdonald who had recovered fully by the time they were back in India, about the forbidding land and the friendly odd people, about his journey back when he saw St. Elmo's fire late one night on the ship, and the time he spent in Italy. But mostly he told her about Sarge and she seemed to listen most intently when he tried to explain some of the things he had learned from his Tibetan friend. He knew he had much to digest, much to sit on, and that it would take years before he fully understood what had happened and could explain it clearly to others. He also sensed that much would never be understood in words.

He also told her of their leave-taking, of how Sarge's dark eyes had looked at him with a look that was profound and simple and sad and full of the joy of life and then his stocky Tibetan shape was ambling down the road back to Lhasa.

Candler told her also of the book he had found in Tibet and then given away in Italy, told her of the temples he had seen and of the many gods whose serene visages he had gazed upon. Told her of the mountains and the snow. He then remembered he had one more thing to tell her, which he decided to do the next day.

The hour was late, the tall clock in the hall chimed once, as Candler continued staring into the fire, now low and hissing quietly. Reaching into the drawer of a table next to his large chair, he removed the package and leaned forward, weighing it in his hand. With quiet respect, he began untying the string.